PRAISE FOR SPUR AWARD–WINNING AUTHOR MATT BRAUN

"Matt Braun is one of the best!"
—Don Coldsmith, author of
THE SPANISH BIT SERIES

"Braun tackles the big men, the complex personalities of
those brave few who were pivotal figures in the
settling of an untamed frontier."
—Jory Sherman, author of
GRASS KINGDOM

"Matt Braun is head and shoulders above all the rest who
would attempt to bring the gunmen of the Old West to life."
—Terry C. Johnston, author of
THE PLAINSMAN SERIES

"Matt Braun has a genius for taking real characters out of the Old
West and giving them flesh-and-blood immediacy."
—Dee Brown, author of
BURY MY HEART AT WOUNDED KNEE

"Braun blends historical fact and ingenious fiction . . .
a top-drawer Western novelist!"
—Robert L. Gale,
Western Biographer

Jury of Six

MATT BRAUN

St. Martin's Paperbacks

This is a work of fiction. All of the characters, organizations, and events portrayed in this novel are either products of the author's imagination or are used fictitiously.

JURY OF SIX

Copyright © 1980 by Matthew Braun.

For information address St. Martin's Press, 175 Fifth Avenue, New York, NY 10010.

ISBN: 978-0-312-98176-1

Printed in the United States of America

Pocket Books edition / May 1980
St. Martin's Paperbacks edition / July 2002

St. Martin's Paperbacks are published by St. Martin's Press, 175 Fifth Avenue, New York, NY 10010.

10 9 8 7 6 5

To Bill
Uncle, friend and Texan

CHAPTER 1

Ben Langham reined to a halt on the north bank of the Canadian. He looped the reins around the saddlehorn and fished a tobacco pouch from inside his greatcoat. His horse lowered its muzzle to the water while he stuffed and lit his pipe.

On the sundown side of sixty, Langham was nonetheless a man of imposing stature. Age had thickened his waistline, but he sat tall in the saddle, head erect and shoulders squared. With a mane of white hair, and wind-seamed features, he looked very much like a grizzled centaur. The pipe jutting from his mouth, he puffed cottony wads of smoke and slowly regarded the sky.

There was a bite in the air, unusually sharp for early December. A heavy overcast screened the afternoon sun, and beyond the river umber plains stretched onward like a burnt-out sea. Shifting in the saddle, Langham tested the wind, searching for the scent of snow. A slight northerly breeze was crisp and dry, but he'd weathered too many storms in the Panhandle not to recognize the signs of oncoming winter. Soon, he told himself, the blizzards would howl down off the high plains and blanket the land with snow. Which meant today might very well be his last chance to inspect the line camps until spring melt-off.

To Langham, the line camps were a hedge that often spelled the difference between disaster and a profitable year. As the largest rancher in the Texas Panhandle, his LX spread was much too big to be manned from the home compound. Like a small nation, it needed outposts during the long plains winter. Spotted every six miles around the fifty-mile perimeter, these outposts formed a fence of sorts on the open range. Cattle had a tendency to drift with a storm, or to mindlessly gather in bunches, shivering and hungry, and starve to death rather than seek out graze. The line riders patrolled between their stations, holding the cows on LX land and driving them to hillsides where wind had blown snow off the grass. A grueling task, it was a job assigned to the most trustworthy men on Langham's crew. Without them, the winter-kill alone would have soon bankrupted the LX.

Yet, while Langham himself had handpicked the line riders, he understood that even the best of men occasionally needed prodding. Life in a line camp, which consisted of a one-room cabin and a log corral, was a solitary existence. With the onset of winter, a line rider often went for weeks at a time without seeing another human. The loneliness and the drudgery of herding stubborn cattle through snowdrifts could sour a man, slowly work on his spirit and turn him lax. A surprise visit and a word of encouragement would do much to bolster that spirit. And the uncertainty, never knowing when to expect another visit, gave the men something to ponder on cold winter nights.

Langham knocked the dottle from his pipe, thoughtful a moment. He was privately amused that the men considered him the original sonofabitch, far more demanding than Jack Noonan, the ranch foreman. At his age it was no small compliment, one he meant to preserve. He nurtured it at every opportunity.

Stuffing the pipe in his pocket, Langham gathered the reins and kneed his horse into the water. Once across the river, he turned west and rode along the shelterbelt of trees bordering the shore. His thoughts now centered on Shorty Phillips, who was stationed at a line camp several miles upstream. He debated staying for supper, then quickly decided against it. No slouch as a cowhand, Phillips's cooking could gag a dog off a gut wagon.

Some while later, Langham crested a wooded knoll and hauled back sharply on the reins. Below, where the treeline thinned out, several riders were hazing a bunch of cows away from the river. At first glance, he thought some of the crew were moving cattle to another section of range. Then he looked closer, and realized none of the men rode for LX. The bastards were cow thieves.

And they were rustling his stock!

Langham reacted instinctively, his hand moving

to the carbine in his saddle scabbard. But blind anger quickly gave way to cool judgment. He counted seven men, and forced himself to admit the odds were too great. He needed help, even if it meant allowing the rustlers to escape for the moment. His mind turned to Shorty Phillips, estimating time and distance. Within the hour he could have Phillips riding for the home compound; another three hours, four at the outside, and Phillips could return with most of the LX crew. By nightfall they would be on the rustlers' trail, and easily overtake them at first light. The conclusion, though delayed, would be no less satisfying. A stiff rope and a short drop always settled a rustler's hash.

The plan formulated, Langham shoved the carbine back in the scabbard and gathered his reins. So intent had he been on the rustlers that the whirr of a gun hammer caught him completely unawares. He turned, scanning the trees to his rear, and found himself staring into the muzzle of a cocked pistol. Not ten yards away a young boy, mounted on a bloodbay gelding, sat watching him over the gunsights. There was a haunting familiarity about the youngster's features, and for an instant the two men stared at each other. Then the boy wagged his head.

"Old man, you're too nosy for your own good."

"You're makin' a mistake," Langham warned him. "No way on God's earth you'll get away with it."

The boy's mouth twisted in a bucktoothed grin. "Wanna bet?"

"Well, I'll be damned." Langham blinked, suddenly recognized the misshapen face he'd seen on reward dodgers. "I know you!"

"Now you done spoiled it for sure."

The boy fired twice, one report blending with the other. Langham swayed, jolted by the impact of the slugs, then slowly toppled out of the saddle. He hit the ground on his side and rolled over, bright dots of blood staining his coat. He groaned, struggling to rise, and somehow levered himself to his hands and knees. His mouth ajar, head hung between his arms, he stared sightlessly at the hard-packed earth. He tried to speak, but produced only a distorted whisper.

The youngster watched his struggles with an expression of detached curiosity. Then he sighted carefully and shot Langham in the head. The rancher's skull exploded in a mist of gore and bone matter, and he collapsed. His leg twitched, and his foot drummed the dirt in a spasm of afterdeath. A moment passed, then he lay still.

At the last shot, his horse spooked, rearing away. The boy aimed, triggering two quick shots, and the horse went down in a tangle of hooves and saddle leather. Without haste, the youngster calmly reloaded and holstered his pistol. Then he reined the bay around and rode down the knoll.

Shorty Phillips discovered the body early next morning. A couple of hours later, still rattled by what he'd seen, he rode into the home compound. There, once Jack Noonan had him calmed down, he spilled out the story. While riding his regular patrol, he had spotted buzzards circling the knoll, and upon investigating, he'd found Langham's body. Other than covering the remains with his mackinaw, he hadn't waited around. He hit the saddle and rode.

The foreman immediately summoned Luke Starbuck. Headquartered at the LX, Starbuck was chief range detective for the Panhandle Cattlemen's Association. The news of Langham's death struck him hard, for he'd been a lifelong friend, and at one time foreman of the LX. But he listened impassively, revealing nothing of what he felt, and questioned Phillips in a cold, measured voice. Then he ordered horses saddled, and sent someone to fetch his assistant, John Poe. Within minutes, Starbuck and Poe, trailed by Noonan and Shorty Phillips, rode out of the compound.

Shortly before noon, the men reined to a halt atop the knoll. Buzzards had already begun working on the dead horse, but took wing as the riders approached. Starbuck sent John Poe to scout the outlying area, and told the other two men to remain with the horses. Then he walked forward and knelt beside Langham's body. When he lifted the mackinaw, his face turned ashen and for a moment it seemed his iron composure would crack. Yet he somehow collected himself and, after inspecting the grisly remains, climbed to his feet. Without a word, he began a careful examination of the knoll.

Noonan and Phillips watched in silence. Neither of them offered to help, for they saw that a quietness had settled over Starbuck. A manhunter for the past four years, tracking down rustlers and horse thieves, he had acquired a reputation for steel nerves and suddenness with a gun. Outlaws seldom surrendered when cornered, and in the time he'd served as a range detective, he was known to have killed eleven men. The number he had hung was a matter of speculation. The nearest peace officer was four days' ride to the south, and summary justice was widely practiced on the plains. Starbuck, according to rumor, had decorated a dozen or more trees throughout the Panhandle. But he was a private man, with no tolerance for questions, and the exact count was unknown. Those who had worked with him, however, told of an eerie quietness he displayed when pushed beyond certain limits. Some men called it a *killing quietness*, and the record seemed to bear them out. Today, watching him, Noonan and Phillips were aware he hadn't spoken since looking underneath the mackinaw.

Starbuck completed his examination as Poe topped the knoll and rode toward them. He waited, his mouth set in a grim line, with Noonan and Phillips standing beside him. When Poe dismounted, he wasted no time on preliminaries.

"How many?"

"I make it seven or eight," Poe informed him. "Found signs where they were drivin' a bunch of cows, then all of a sudden they just stopped and hightailed it out of here."

"Figures," Starbuck observed. "One of them was posted up here as a lookout. The way I read it, Ben rode in from the north, and when he saw what was happening, the lookout killed him."

"So they ditched the cows to make better time. Whoever's leadin' them evidently wanted to be long gone by the time Ben was found."

"That's how it adds up."

"Ben have any chance at all?"

"None," Starbuck said tonelessly. "Bastard drilled him twice, then finished him off with one in the head. No way of telling, but I'd say he shot the horse so it wouldn't show up with an empty saddle and raise an alarm. Probably figured that'd buy them a little more time."

"That, or he's plain kill crazy."

"Crazy like a fox." Starbuck extended his hand, five spent cartridges cupped in his palm. "Found these over in the trees. He sat there and reloaded before he rode off. That tell you anything?"

"Offhand, I'd say he's not the type that spooks easy."

"Yeah, that's for sure." Starbuck paused, considering. "How about tracks?"

"I followed them maybe half a mile, no trouble."

"Which direction?"

"Southwest," Poe noted. "Straight as a string."

Starbuck nodded. "New Mexico."

"You thinkin' what I'm thinkin'?"

"Maybe, maybe not; but I know a place we can find out."

Late that night, Starbuck and Poe rode into Tascosa. An isolated trading post, the town was situated on the Canadian River, roughly halfway between LX lands and the eastern border of New Mexico. Apart from a few adobes, there was one saloon and a general store. Tascosa had no streets, only a handful of permanent residents, and no law. It was the perfect haven for outlaws, on the edge of nowhere.

When Starbuck pushed through the batwing doors, a measurable hush fell over the saloon. There were perhaps a dozen men standing at the bar and seated around crude tables. Some of them knew him on sight, and the others would have instantly recognized his name. Yet, even to those who had never seen him, his presence was a matter to be weighed with care. In Tascosa, where every man looked to his own safety, caution was the basic tenet of survival.

With Poe at his side, Starbuck walked directly to the bar. Outside, he had checked the horses tied at the hitch rack, and none of them had been ridden hard. A swift glance around the saloon further strengthened his hunch: the men he sought were by now across the border into New Mexico. He rapped on the counter, and the bartender hurried forward.

"Evenin', Mr. Starbuck."

"Ernie." Starbuck nodded amiably. "How's tricks?"

"Oh, you know, dollar here, dollar there. What can I get you gents?"

"A little information."

The barkeep gave him a guarded look. "I try to tend to my own knittin', Mr. Starbuck. Feller stays healthier that way."

"Ernie, you've got a choice." Starbuck paused, motioning around the room. "You can worry about these boys later, or you can worry about me now. Which way you want it?"

"Jesus." The barkeep licked his lips, shot a nervous glance over his shoulder. "That ain't no choice at all."

"Wasn't meant to be." Starbuck fixed him with a level gaze. "Last night, maybe the night before, eight men wandered in here for a drink. Tell me about them."

"How'd you hear about that bunch?"

"Let's stick to me asking the questions."

"Well, there's not nothin' special to tell, except maybe . . ."

"Yeah," Starbuck prompted him, "except maybe what?"

"The youngest one," the barkeep replied thoughtfully. "No more'n a kid, but the others treated him like he was meaner than tiger spit. Sorta strange."

"Describe him," Starbuck persisted. "Anything you remember."

"Oh, he was an ugly little scutter. Wouldn't stand

no taller'n your shoulder. And his face was all lop-sided. Looked like a jackrabbit when he grinned."

"You mean he was bucktoothed?"

"Near about as bad as I ever seen."

Starbuck turned to Poe. "What do you say, John? Think he fits the ticket?"

"In spades!" Poe agreed. "Couldn't be no one else."

"And I'll bet they called him Billy." Starbuck pinned the barkeep with a look. "Didn't they, Ernie?"

"How the hell'd you know that?"

"Took a wild guess." Starbuck stepped away from the bar. His eyes traveled around the room, moving from face to face. "This here's private business, just between me and Ernie. Anybody sees it different, now's the time to speak his piece."

A leaden stillness filled the saloon. None of the men spoke, and no one met Starbuck's gaze. After a brief while he dug a double eagle from his pocket and tossed it on the counter.

"A drink for my friends, Ernie."

Starbuck walked to the door. He waited there, watching the room, until John Poe was outside. Then he stepped into the night. A moment later the sound of hoofbeats slowly faded from Tascosa.

CHAPTER 2

Ben Langham was buried the next afternoon. His casket was borne to the graveyard by six cowhands. A few steps behind the pallbearers, Starbuck followed with Jack Noonan and John Poe. Several cattlemen, whose ranches bordered the LX, brought up the rear.

The procession entered the small cemetery north of the compound and halted. The casket was lowered onto planks laid across the grave, then the pallbearers stepped back and the men removed their hats. Vernon Pryor, one of the ranchers, walked to the head of the grave. Except for itinerant preachers, religion was a sometimes thing in the Panhandle; funeral services were always kept simple, the last words spoken by a close friend. Pryor opened a dog-eared Bible and began reading the Twenty-third Psalm.

Starbuck scarcely heard the words. The service was properly somber, and some ninety cowhands, almost all the LX crew, were gathered around the cemetery. But for him there was a sense of the unreal about the burial. He stared at a coffin which represented nothing, merely a rough-hewn wooden box. His mind was suspended in a void of bygone years, and he saw revealed there an image of all that had once been and would never be again. His grief, even now tightly suppressed, had not yet come to grips with an essential truth. Ben Langham was dead.

To him, there had always been a godlike quality about Langham. Olympian in manner, a white-haired monolith, the rancher had seemed indestructible. Other men lived and died, but Ben Langham went on forever, ageless and somehow immutable. Starbuck saw him that way still.

Some ten years past, Starbuck had hired on as a trailhand with the LX. A drifter, wandering the aimless life of a saddle tramp, he was a nomad without family or roots. But Langham, who was a keen judge of character, quickly brought a halt to his wanderlust. Assuming ever greater responsibility, Starbuck was promoted to head wrangler, and then jumped to trail boss a year later. Within three seasons, he went from fiddle-footed cowhand to segundo of the LX.

At the time, Langham's spread was located in the Rio Grande Valley, near the Mexican border. During the summer of 1874, however, tragedy struck the ranch. An outbreak of cholera claimed the lives of Langham's wife and three children, along with a score of cowhands. Devastated by the loss, and determined to outdistance memories of the past, Langham turned his gaze north, to the Texas Panhandle.

There, on the banks of the Canadian River, he established a new ranch. But he brought with him the LX brand and Luke Starbuck, who assumed the post of foreman.

Thereafter, a sense of closeness and kinship steadily developed between Langham and Starbuck. The old man looked on his young foreman with affection and pride, much as a father would treat a son. Working together, they created a prosperous ranch out of a raw wilderness. By the spring of 1876, the LX was running fifty thousand head of cattle and the crew numbered nearly a hundred men. That summer ten herds went up the trail to railhead, and the proceeds to the ranch totaled in excess of a half million dollars. Ben Langham, within the space of two years, had become the most influential stockgrower in the Panhandle. And he was quick to credit his foreman with having converted an ocean of grass into a top-notch cattle outfit.

Yet the summer of '76 had proved a crossroads in Luke Starbuck's life. Besieged by rustlers and horse thieves, the Panhandle Cattlemen's Association had been forced to take action. At Langham's urging, Starbuck had been appointed the Association's first range detective. His orders were to run the outlaws to earth, wherever the trail might lead, and see justice done. Since vast distances and poor communications stymied elected peace officers, his mandate from the Association gave him the power of judge, jury, and executioner. He was hindered neither by state boundaries nor the law itself, for the renegade bands respected no code except that imposed at the end of a gun. His credentials as a detective were quickly established, and with each outlaw hung or killed, his reputation took on added luster. Still, no sooner was one gang routed than another appeared to take its place, and what began as a temporary assignment evolved into a deadly vocation. He became a professional manhunter.

Over the past four years, Starbuck had grown cold and hard, brutalized by the sight of death. Today, staring at Ben Langham's coffin, he mourned the passing of a man who had befriended him and taught him the meaning of family. But his grief was inward, a white-hot coal that burned to the very core of his vitals. Outwardly he was stoic, somehow dispassionate, and curiously uninvolved in the ancient rites of burial. His thoughts were not of remorse, but of revenge.

Vernon Pryor finished reading and closed his Bible. Starbuck caught only the last few words, then the sound of ropes sawing on wood jarred him back to the present. He blinked and saw the pallbearers lowering the coffin into the ground. He forced himself to watch, but his mind was focused on the task ahead. As the top of the coffin disappeared, there was a moment of strained silence. Then, jamming his hat on his head, he turned away from the grave.

The four ranchers, all older men, immediately stepped forward to shake his hand. Each in turn offered condolences and expressed his sorrow, for it was widely known that Ben Langham had considered Starbuck the same as family. Their remarks were accepted without comment, and then, his voice deliberate, Starbuck addressed them as a group.

"We've got some things that need talking out. As long as you're here, I'd like to call a special meeting of the Association."

A statement rather than a request, his tone left the ranchers momentarily flustered. Before anyone could reply, he stepped past them and moved away. Outside the cemetery plot, the LX hands kept their heads bowed, their eyes averted. His expression was stony, and he looked straight ahead as they opened a path before him. A solitary figure, withdrawn into himself, he walked toward the main house.

Starbuck was waiting when they filed into the office. The ranchers were uncomfortably aware that he stood behind Ben Langham's desk. For several years, seated at that desk, the LX owner had ruled the Panhandle Cattlemen's Association. An aura of power still lingered in the room, and the men exchanged uneasy glances as they moved forward. Starbuck motioned them to chairs.

"Suppose we get to it," he said brusquely. "I'm short on time, but I thought it only fair that I advise you of a couple of things. One's got to do with the LX, and the other involves the Association."

Vernon Pryor and Will Rutledge were seated directly across from him. Oscar Gilchrist and Earl Musgrave had taken chairs at either end of the desk.

Early settlers in the Panhandle, they had established their own ranches shortly after Ben Langham staked out the LX. Yet, while they admired Langham, their feelings were mixed about Starbuck. In the beginning, he had earned their respect as ramrod of the LX; though not yet thirty, his knowledge of cows, and general ranch operations, surpassed that of men twice his age. Later, as a range detective, his methods had often disturbed them. He obtained results, but the ranchers were of the opinion that he overstepped himself, frequently exceeding his authority. Only Langham had been able to hold him in check, and now that steadying influence was gone. The prospect unnerved them more than they cared to admit.

Vernon Pryor cleared his throat. A man of glacial calm, he was tall and distinguished, and the other men attached a certain importance to his views. Over the years, whenever they were at odds with Langham, he had acted as their spokesman. Now, his fingers steepled, he peered across the desk at Starbuck.

"Luke, you seem to have us at a disadvantage."

"How so?"

"Well, for one thing," Pryor replied, "we'd like to know your position here today. Are you talking for the LX, or have you asked us here in your official capacity with the Association?"

"Both." Starbuck took a one-page document from the desk drawer and laid it before them. "For openers, there's Ben's last will and testament. It's right to the point, so you might as well read it for your-selves."

While the ranchers huddled around the will, Star-buck pulled out the makings and began rolling himself a smoke. The document, like the man who had written it, was blunt and without equivocation. The ranchers evidenced no great surprise as they read, and it required less than a minute for them to scan the contents. Starbuck struck a match and lit his cigarette, waiting until they looked up.

"Ben wasn't much with words," he said quietly, "but I reckon he spelled it out pretty clear."

"Very clear," Pryor remarked. "According to this, you inherit everything he owned. No exceptions and no conditions. You're to be congratulated, Luke."

"Damned right!" Earl Musgrave added. "Ben always said you was like blood kin, and by Christ, he wasn't kiddin'."

The other men quickly endorsed the sentiment. By conservative estimate, Starbuck was now a man of enviable wealth. Then too, ownership of the LX conferred on him a mantle of power, for it was the largest, and easily the most prosperous, cattle operation in the Panhandle. That fact wasn't lost on the ranchers, and it did nothing to quell their apprehension.

Starbuck sensed their concern. "You needn't worry about me trying to fill Ben's boots. I only showed you the will so we'd have all our cards on the table. That and nothing else."

"Pardon me," Pryor said, tapping the will. "I notice this is dated May 1, 1876. If I'm not mistaken, that's about the time you accepted your first assignment as a range detective."

"To peg it exact, it was one day after I accepted."

"In other words," Pryor commented, "he told you about the will the day he wrote it."

Starbuck took a long drag on his cigarette. He exhaled, watching the rancher, and slowly nodded. "Ben always liked to sandbag the odds. He decided the Association needed me more than the ranch, but he wanted to make sure I'd stick around—and take over—after he was gone." He paused, inspecting his cigarette, then shrugged. "I guess he figured only a damn fool would walk away from a deal like that."

"Was he right?"

"Why do you ask?"

"Oh, nothing." Pryor gave him a crafty smile. "It's just that I get the feeling you're not all that concerned with the LX."

"Maybe later," Starbuck told him, "but not now. Tomorrow I'm headed for New Mexico."

"New Mexico!" Gilchrist blurted. "What the hell's in New Mexico?"

"The fellow that killed Ben."

A pall fell over the ranchers. Starbuck walked to the window and stood staring out at the compound. Briefly, he related the details of his search at the knoll, and then went on to describe what he'd uncovered in Tascosa. When he turned away from the window, his eyes were dulled and a small knot pulsed at his temple.

"Put it all together, and it spells the same name every time. Billy the Kid."

"Billy the Kid!"

Will Rutledge trumpeted the name, but the other ranchers were no less astounded. All four men shifted in their chairs, gaping at Starbuck, and for an instant they appeared struck dumb. Then Oscar Gilchrist found his voice.

"You can't do it, Luke. Gawddamnit, we won't let you do it! You're head of the LX now, and we need you here."

"Oscar's right," Musgrave chimed in. "It's too risky. Hell's fire, they're still fightin' the Lincoln County War! You get yourself mixed up in that and you're liable to wind up in New Mexico permanent."

"Save your breath," Starbuck said flatly. "I should have gone after the Kid a long time ago. If I had, Ben would be alive today."

"Judas Priest!" Musgrave protested. "It was Ben that always stopped you! I heard him myself, sittin' right there behind that desk. He told you to stay the hell out of New Mexico till they quit squabblin' amongst themselves. Ain't that so?"

"Hold on, Earl," Pryor temporized. "Maybe Luke has a point. For all practical purposes, the Lincoln County War is over and done with. I even hear they've got themselves a new sheriff. So maybe now's the time to rid ourselves of the Kid once and for all."

"One thing's for sure," Rutledge interjected.

"The little bastard knows Luke's got orders not to cross the state line. Hell, he has to know! That's why him and his gang keep hittin' our herds so regular."

Starbuck's mouth hardened. "Those orders died with Ben. Tomorrow, I'm heading out with John Poe and three or four good men. We'll stay till we get the job done."

"I still don't like it," Gilchrist said dourly. "New Mexico ain't like other places, Luke. Them people has turned killin' one another into a sport, and an outsider wouldn't have no more chance than spit on a hot stove."

"Oscar, you could talk yourself blue in the face, but it won't change a thing. I'm going, and the argument stops there."

"What about the LX?" Pryor ventured. "I know you feel bound to go after Ben's killer, but there's always the chance you won't come back. Have you thought about that?"

Starbuck's laugh was scratchy, abrasive. "Tell you what, Vern. If somebody punches my ticket, I won't have much use for the LX. You boys can divvy it up any way you please."

"Would you put that in writing?"

"Gawddamn, Vern!" Gilchrist admonished him. "You sound like you already got Luke measured for a pine box."

"No, he's right," Starbuck admitted. "Anything happens to me, it wouldn't be legal unless it was in writing." He hesitated, eyes squinted in a sardonic look. "Course, there's something I'd want in exchange."

"Oh?" Pryor said slowly. "What's that?"

"A letter of authorization from the Association."

"Dead or alive?" Pryor asked. "For Billy the Kid?"

"Why not?" Starbuck smiled. "Word it right, and it might just keep the law off my neck."

The ranchers glanced quickly at each other. It seemed a reasonable request, and while they wished Starbuck no harm, all of them were acutely aware that a new element had been introduced into the discussion. His death would profit them handsomely, and every man was obliged to look to his own interests. At length, Pryor nodded, once more the spokesman.

"Agreed," he said evenly. "But if I was you, I'd pay a call on John Chisum. He's president of the New Mexico Stockgrowers' Association, and it wouldn't hurt to have his support. If you like, I'll even write him a personal note."

"Which side of the fence is he on?"

"The winning side! Matter of fact, I hear tell he handpicked their new sheriff. Fellow by the name of Pat Garrett."

"Never heard of him." Starbuck stubbed out his cigarette in an ashtray, thoughtful a moment. "All right, I'll see what Chisum has to say for himself. But whichever way it goes, I still aim to get the Kid."

"Don't go off half-cocked," Pryor advised. "John

Chisum makes a lot better friend than he does an enemy."

"Well, Vern, I reckon that'll be up to him."

"Meaning you intend to play it your own way, regardless?"

Starbuck smiled. "What the hell, why spoil a perfect record?"

CHAPTER 3

On December 8, Starbuck forded the Pecos River. He was accompanied by John Poe and four LX cowhands. The men were a rough lot, all of them veterans of previous manhunts and intensely loyal to Starbuck. Once across the river, they turned south and rode toward the Jinglebob Ranch.

Starbuck now regretted his promise to call on John Chisum. Three days in the saddle had afforded time to think it through, and he questioned that anything worthwhile would come of the meeting. He'd dealt with cattle barons before, and Chisum, who was known as the King of the Pecos, would very likely try to exert some form of control over his actions. But he was determined to operate on his own, without constraint and answerable to no one. His purpose was to exact simple vengeance—an eye for an eye—uncomplicated by courts or legal technicalities. He foresaw problems ahead.

Late that afternoon, Starbuck and his men sighted the Jinglebob headquarters. Located in the southeastern quadrant of New Mexico Territory, the ranch was a day's ride from the town of Lincoln.

Everything about the Jinglebob was mammoth in scope. Natural landmarks, such as rivers and mountains, were used to measure its boundary lines. Over 100,000 cows grazed its range, and a crew of one hundred fifty cowhands was kept on the payroll year round. Thirty years before, John Chisum had laid claim to a sprawling empire, defending it against outlaws and marauding Indians, and successive waves of westward-bound settlers. A man who recognized no authority but his own, he ruled the Pecos like a feudal lord.

The *casa grande* was of a style befitting the man and his ranch. It was one story, constructed of native adobe, with broad wings extending off the central living quarters. Beneath a tile roof, hewn beams protruded from walls four feet thick. The window casements gleamed of tallowed oak, and the double doors were wider than a man's outspanned arms. The house, which overlooked the river to the west, dominated the ranch compound. Covering several acres, the buildings were grouped with a symmetry that was at once methodical and pleasing to the eye. Four bunkhouses formed a quadrangle, with a dining hall the size of an army barracks in the center. Corrals and stables, flanked by a line of storage buildings, angled south along a bend in the river. A commissary and an open-sided blacksmith shed were situated on a plot of open ground central to the entire compound. The effect was that of a small but prosperous village, bustling with activity.

All afternoon, since crossing the Jinglebob

boundary, Starbuck had expected to be challenged. A group of six strangers, appearing unannounced on open rangeland, was a matter to warrant questions. But no one had approached them, and now, as they rode across the compound, their presence attracted little more than passing interest. At the hitchrack, Starbuck and his men dismounted. He left Poe in charge, ordering them to stay with the horses until he returned. Then he walked toward the main house.

Before he could knock, the doors swung open. A girl, dressed rather formally in a lavender taffeta gown, stood just inside the entranceway. Her smile was tentative, and she fixed him with a steady, inquiring gaze.

"Good afternoon."

"Ma'am." Starbuck doffed his hat. "I wonder if I might have a word with Mr. Chisum?"

"Of course." She stepped aside, motioning him into the vestibule. "My father has been expecting you for some time."

Starbuck moved past her, struck by both her words and her unusual beauty. She had dark eyes and high cheekbones and raven hair wound in coils atop her head. Her skin was soft and creamy, untouched by wind or sun, and her mouth was a lovely oval. She was small and compact, with a stemlike waist and breasts that formed perfect mounds. She seemed to him something out of a storybook, ethereal and strangely out of place. As she closed the doors, he collected himself, turned to face her.

"Excuse my manners," he said, smiling. "I

should've introduced myself right off. I'm Luke Starbuck."

"Mr. Starbuck." She nodded pleasantly. "My name is Sallie Chisum."

Starbuck scarcely heard the words. Her voice was intimate, with the timbre of an old violin. Yet it was a trained voice, very proper and very correct. His head buzzed with questions, but he restrained himself.

"Pleasure, Miss Chisum. If you'll pardon my saying so, you sort of took me by surprise. We don't often see ladies like you over my way."

"Oh?" Sallie Chisum said, watching him. "And where is that, Mr. Starbuck?"

"The Panhandle," he replied. "North of Palo Duro Canyon."

"You've ridden a long way."

"Yes, ma'am, that's a fact."

"May I ask why you wish to see my father?"

"A business matter," Starbuck noted vaguely. "I represent the Cattlemen's Association."

"I see."

She paused, waiting for him to elaborate, but instead Starbuck's eyebrows lifted in question. "You say your father was expecting me?"

"Yes, indeed," she explained, suddenly amused. "You and your men have been under observation from the moment you rode onto Jinglebob. Father is about to perish of curiosity."

"Sounds like your hands keep their eyes open."

She merely smiled, indicating a hallway. "Shall

we? I suspect father's patience has about reached its limit."

"Oh, sure thing." Starbuck took a step back. "After you."

Sallie Chisum led him down the corridor. She walked quickly, with a sort of bustling vitality, and the rustle of silk seemed pitted in counterpoint to the clink of his spurs on the tiled floor. He was abruptly aware of the bearded stubble on his jaws, and the layer of trail dust covering his clothes. The delicate scent of her perfume made him wonder if he smelled as rank as he looked. He felt very much like a moth swooping along behind a butterfly.

At the end of the hall, she went through an open door and stopped. Starbuck entered, and found himself in a combination office-den. There was an odor of tobacco and saddle leather, and flames crackled in the fireplace. A massive desk occupied one side of the room, with a stuffed eagle mounted on a pedestal and gun racks lining the walls. Opposite the desk, directly before the fireplace, an old man sat slumped in a wing chair.

"Father," Sallie Chisum said graciously, "we have a guest. Mr. Starbuck, of the Panhandle Cattlemen's Association."

"Mr. Chisum." Starbuck crossed the room, his hand extended. "I'm Luke Starbuck."

"Welcome to Jinglebob." Chisum shook hands without rising, then motioned him to a companion wing chair. "Take a load off your feet."

While Starbuck removed his mackinaw, the girl

28

turned and walked to the door. She smiled, nodding to him, and looked at her father.

"If you need anything, I'll be in the parlor."

The door closed, and Chisum waited until he had seated himself. After a moment, the rancher waved a square, stubby-fingered hand toward a wall cabinet.

"Care for a whiskey?"

"No, thanks."

"Coffee?"

"Much obliged, but I'll pass."

"Luke Starbuck." Chisum's cordial manner became a swift look of appraisal. "I don't know you, but I know your name."

Starbuck shrugged. "I reckon bad news travels fastest."

"Well, I sort of like what I've heard so far. But, then, I get the feelin' I ain't heard it all. What's your business with Jinglebob?"

"Here." Starbuck dug out a soiled envelope and passed it to him. "That's from Vernon Pryor. He told me to tell you it'd pretty much explain things."

Chisum pulled metal-framed spectacles from his shirt pocket, tore open the envelope, and began reading. Starbuck studied him, betraying nothing, but frankly astounded by the rancher's appearance. A withered giant, his features were those of a fleshed skeleton bound with gray, chalky skin. He was completely bald, with bone china teeth, and he spoke with the slurred inflections of a man wasted by illness. Only his eyes were alive, and by exercise of sheer will, his mind remained attentive. Starbuck thought to himself that time was the cruelest of vandals. Other contests might end in a draw, but John Chisum had already lost his struggle with the years.

When he finished the letter, Chisum folded his spectacles and returned them to his pocket. He cleared his throat, slowly shook his head.

"Sorry about Langham. Our trails never crossed, but I always heard good things about him. Damn shame he had to get it that way."

Starbuck nodded. "He deserved better."

Chisum fell silent. He saw in Starbuck's cold, slate-colored eyes the look of a man who stayed alive by making quick estimates. He himself was no mean judge of character, and he sensed that accounts of Starbuck's work as a manhunter were in no way exaggerated. He speculated on the possibilities, weighing his next words carefully. At length, he tapped the letter with his finger.

"According to Pryor, you aim to run the Kid down and kill him."

"Yeah, I guess that's about the size of it."

"What about his gang?" Chisum asked. "Aren't you interested in getting them?"

"All things evened out, I'd be satisfied with the Kid."

"Well, Mr. Starbuck, the plain fact of the matter is—I wouldn't!"

Starbuck met his gaze. "I get the feeling you're trying to tell me something."

"Would it surprise you," Chisum said bitterly, "to

learn that the Kid and his gang only spend half their time in the Panhandle? The rest of the time they're figurin' out ways to rustle Jinglebob cows."

"If that's the case, why haven't you put a stop to it? You've got enough men on your payroll."

"Humph!" Chisum grunted. "Lemme ask you something, Starbuck. How much do you know about the Lincoln County War?"

"Not a whole lot."

"Then it's time somebody gave you an earful. Otherwise you won't get no closer to the Kid than we have."

Chisum quickly sketched events of the past three years. Essentially a political struggle, the Lincoln County War involved two factions. On one side were Chisum and another rancher, John Tunstall, and a local storekeeper, Alexander McSween. Challenging them were L. G. Murphy and his partner, Jack Dobson, whose interests included a ranch as well as the town's leading business establishments. More than twenty men had met their deaths during the fighting, including Tunstall, McSween, and L. G. Murphy. Several of them had been murdered in cold blood by Billy the Kid, who worked for Tunstall and McSween even though he detested Chisum. After the fighting had subsided, Chisum made his peace with Jack Dobson. Their compromise was a simple division of the spoils: Dobson controlled the town government and Chisum assumed command of county politics. Ironically, the truce transformed Billy the Kid from a hired gun into an outlaw leader. He vilified Chisum for having compromised, and quickly formed a gang of murderous renegades. For the last year, the Kid and his men had raided Jinglebob herds on an average of once a month.

"Small ranchers," Chisum concluded, "and especially the Mexicans, think the Kid's some sort of Robin Hood. Course, him robbing the rich to help the poor ain't nothin' but a load of horseshit! But they believe it—and they protect him—and catchin' the little bastard's like trying to grab a puff of smoke."

Starbuck considered a moment. "I was told you got your own man elected sheriff. What's he done about the Kid?"

"Not a goddamn thing!" Chisum said sternly. "Now, don't misunderstand me. Pat Garrett's a regular bulldog, and he's honest as they come. But so far he ain't cut the mustard as a lawman."

"Then why'd you put him in office?"

"Cause I could trust him," Chisum countered. "On top of which, he used to be pals with the Kid. Nothin' illegal, but they was real thick, and there ain't nobody knows the Kid better'n Pat Garrett. So he seemed like a natural."

Starbuck looked skeptical. "What's your point? You wouldn't be telling me all this unless you had a reason. Why not just get to it?"

"Awright," Chisum said gravely. "I've got a bum ticker. Already had two strokes and the Doc says I could go at any time."

"Sorry to hear it," Starbuck said with genuine concern. "But I still don't see your point."

"There's two things I want done before I cash in. I want my daughter married off to a decent man, and I want this rustlin' stopped cold. That's all it'd take for me to go out with the biggest goddamn grin anybody ever seen."

"Well, I'm sure no prospect as a son-in-law, so we must be talking about rustlers."

"What we're talkin' about," Chisum said firmly, "is exterminating the Kid *and* his gang. But I want it done before I die! Otherwise I wouldn't rest easy for fear Sallie might lose everything I've worked a lifetime to build."

Starbuck thought it sounded a bit flimsy. Some inner voice warned him that Chisum wasn't telling the whole story. Then, wondering if perhaps it wasn't his cynical streak at work, he decided to reserve judgment. He rocked his hand back and forth, fingers splayed.

"I see your drift, but you'll have to spell it out a little plainer."

"Nothin' real complicated," Chisum said with an affable gesture. "You're an experienced manhunter and Pat Garrett ain't. If you was to team up with him, I got an idea we'd get this thing settled muy damn pronto."

"I work alone," Starbuck remarked. "Not that I don't need help now and then, but I prefer to use my own men."

"Here in New Mexico, things would go a lot

smoother if you went about it legal. That's no threat; I'm just sayin' folks are still jumpy about strangers, what with all the trouble we've had the last few years. You let Garrett pin a deputy's badge on you, and you'll save yourself a world of grief."

Starbuck laughed. "You'll have to give me a better reason than that. I never needed a tin star before, and I don't see the need now."

A wintry smile lighted the old man's eyes. "Suppose Ben Langham was sittin' here today. Now, like I said, we never met, but unless I miss my guess, he'd tell you to take all the odds you can get. Course, maybe I'm all wet, but I figure that's just the way he would've put it to you."

Starbuck was silent for a long while. At last, still uneasy about Chisum's motives, he inclined his head in a faint nod. "I'll agree on two conditions. First, Garrett has to give me a free hand. So far as anyone else will know, he's still top dog. But either I do it my own way, or I don't do it at all. Second, he has to deputize my men. I trust them, and when the time comes, I want to make damn sure they're backing my play."

"Deal!" Chisum agreed without hesitation. "I'll write him a note and send it into town first thing tomorrow. More'n likely he'll bow his neck, but there won't be no problem. He'll go along."

"Fine." Starbuck uncoiled from his chair and stood. "I'll take it slow on the way into Lincoln. By the time me and the boys get there, maybe Garrett will have simmered down."

"Any idea where you'll start?"

Starbuck gave him a cryptic smile. "Downwind. Anybody that stinks as bad as the Kid, the smell's got to be plumb ripe."

CHAPTER 4

A brilliant sunset edged toward the mountains west of Lincoln. Entering town from the opposite direction, Starbuck was struck by the picturesque setting. To a stranger, unfamiliar with its history of bloodshed and violence, it would have appeared a peaceful community, thriving with commerce.

With John Poe at his side and the men strung out behind, Starbuck inspected the town's main thoroughfare. They rode past an adobe church, with a high bell tower, then the courthouse and several small establishments. A large general store, apparently the only one in Lincoln, dominated the business district. Nearby was a bank and a hotel; farther down the street were shops and saloons and a couple of cafes. Across from one saloon was a burnt-out ruin, obviously a structure of some substance before being reduced to charred rubble. Many of the buildings, notably the hotel and the general store, were pocked with bullet holes.

Starbuck reined to a halt before the hotel. He left Poe with instructions to get the men quartered and the horses stabled. Then he crossed the street and walked back along the boardwalk to the courthouse.

Only last night John Chisum had given him a brief rundown on Lincoln County's new sheriff. After a pleasant supper, seated once again in the den, Starbuck had sipped whiskey and listened while the rancher talked. Pat Garrett had drifted into New Mexico Territory not quite three years past. A former buffalo hunter and cowhand, he quickly evidenced the determination to settle down and make something of himself. With money he'd saved, he opened a saloon at Fort Sumner, and shortly afterwards, he married a local girl. Billy the Kid often frequented his saloon, and in time a friendship developed. The natives jokingly called them "Big Casino" and "Little Casino," for at six-four, Garrett was nearly a foot taller than the Kid. But Garrett had aspirations to bigger things; early in 1880 he moved his family to Roswell, and opened a general store. There he courted the respectable element, businessmen and politicians, and the most influential rancher in the territory, John Chisum. Backed by the Jinglebob owner for sheriff, he had won a landslide victory in the November elections. His one campaign promise was to rid New Mexico of its boy outlaw.

Yet, according to Chisum, the new sheriff had made little headway in the month since the election. There was talk he never would, due to his past friendship with the Kid. Chisum discounted such gossip, however, for he had satisfied himself that Pat Garrett was an ambitious man. One perfectly willing to use the Kid as a steppingstone into the larger arena of territorial politics.

A good listener, Starbuck had nodded and sipped his whiskey and offered no comment. He'd learned long ago that secondhand information was unreliable at best, and all too often misleading. Chisum's assessment of Garrett might very well prove correct. On the other hand, it was entirely possible the town gossips had stumbled upon the truth. So far as Starbuck was concerned, it was a toss of the dice, and a poor bet either way. But now, as he entered the courthouse and moved toward the sheriff's office, he had no qualms. Within a few minutes, he would determine the only truth that mattered. His truth.

Pat Garrett greeted him affably. Expecting resentment, Starbuck was immediately put on guard. But the sheriff pumped his hand, offering him a chair, to all appearances genuinely cordial. Once they were seated, Garrett took a sheet of paper from his desk drawer. He grinned, casually tossing it across the desk.

"I don't know whether you read it or not, but Chisum's letter sure don't mince words. He must've thought the idea would put my nose out of joint."

Starbuck merely glanced at the letter. "You're not sore?"

"Hell, no!" Garrett said earnestly. "I got more troubles than I can say grace over. Besides which, nobody ever accused me of being a dimdot."

"I don't follow you."

"Well, it's no secret that politics put me in office.

Politics and John Chisum. So there's no way I'm gonna start riding a high horse where he's concerned."

"That's it?" Starbuck prompted him. "One hand washes the other, and no questions asked?"

"Not altogether," Garrett replied. "See, I've got a long ways to go as a lawman. I figure you can help me get there, and I'd be a damn fool not to grab the chance. Boiled down, you've got the savvy and I need it. It's just that simple."

Starbuck wondered at the man's candor. Somehow his openness and mild tone didn't square with his rawboned looks. Aside from his towering height, he was broad-shouldered and full through the chest. His features were angular, with wide-set eyes and a straight mouth partially covered by a brushy mustache. All in all, he appeared tough as rawhide, hardly the amiable, easygoing giant. Starbuck thought he would bear watching.

"You're agreeable, then," Starbuck asked at length, "to me calling the shots? No bones now, no bones later?"

"Not a one," Garrett affirmed. "We both want the Kid hung, and for my money, that's all that counts. You've got your reasons and I've got mine—fair enough?"

"Fair enough." Starbuck took out the makings and began rolling a smoke. "Suppose you tell me about the Kid."

"There's not a helluva lot to tell."

"Start with his habits. Other than rustling cows

and killing people, what's he do in his spare time?"

"Oh, he's got the usual vices. Next to liquor and gamblin', he's always had an eye for women."

"Has he got a favorite hangout?"

"A couple," Garrett acknowledged. "Mesilla and Fort Sumner. But he's tricky, always on the move. No way to predict where he'll turn up next."

"Mesilla?" Starbuck struck a match, lit his cigarette. "I seem to recollect that's down near the border."

"Half a day's ride, maybe less."

"Any chance he holes up in Old Mexico after a job?"

"Hell, what's the need? Except for lawmen, he's got no worries north of the border."

"Most folks just naturally take his side, that it?"

"Some do, and them that don't are too scared to let on otherwise. Live and let live, that's their motto."

"Have you ever come close to nailing him?"

"No," Garrett admitted. "He's had me runnin' around like a fart in a bottle, and that's a plain fact. Course, maybe Chisum told you, I've only been in office a little more than a month."

"You mean to say nobody's spotted him? No reports at all?"

"Well—" Garret paused, obviously troubled. "Couple of weeks ago, him and his gang had a brush with the law over around White Oaks. But it was one in a million, strictly an accident. He got away without a scratch."

"Where's White Oaks?"

"Other side of the mountains; northwest of here."

"Northwest." Starbuck pondered a moment. "Suppose the Kid wanted to avoid Lincoln and the Jinglebob. Could he circle around the mountains and cut across to Fort Sumner?"

"Yeah, that'd be one way to do it."

"And from there, he'd have a straight run into the Panhandle, wouldn't he?"

"What're you gettin' at?"

"Nothing," Starbuck said quietly. "Just working my way backwards."

"Backwards to what?"

"Good question." Starbuck made an empty gesture with his hands. "Any idea where the Kid unloads all that rustled stock?"

"God A'mighty!" Garrett snorted. "If I knew that, we wouldn't have no problem, would we?"

"But it has to be someplace close around. Otherwise it doesn't make sense."

"Why do you say that?"

"Because he switches back and forth raiding Chisum and the Panhandle outfits."

"I don't see the connection."

"You would if you had to drive Jinglebob cows over any distance. He has to get rid of them in a hurry, and that means whoever he deals with probably buys everything he rustles."

"Panhandle stock included?"

"Sounds reasonable to me."

"So where does that lead us?"

41

Starbuck almost told him. Then, on sudden impulse, he changed his mind. "Maybe nowhere. I'll have to think on it awhile."

Garrett heaved himself to his feet. "If there's any heavy thinkin' to be done, I always say a man does it better with a drink in his hand. Care to join me?"

"Thanks, Sheriff." Starbuck rose. "Don't mind if I do."

"Call me Pat." Circling the desk, Garrett grinned broadly. "Hell, since I started politickin', I don't hardly answer to nothing else."

"Sure thing," Starbuck said without irony. "My friends call me Luke."

"Well, Luke, let's go get ourselves a dose of pop-skull."

Outside, the men turned west, angling across the street. As they walked, Garrett pointed out the charred ruin, explaining that it had once been the McSween Mercantile. With some relish, he went on to recount the end of the Lincoln County War.

Later dubbed the Three Day Battle, it began when the Kid led a band of hired guns into Lincoln. A direct challenge to the Murphy forces, it was designed to force a showdown. The Kid and his men took cover in the McSween Mercantile and the home that adjoined the store. The opposition, led by Sheriff George Peppin, occupied a store and hotel owned by Murphy and his partner, Jack Dobson. The battle raged for three days and two nights, with gunfire sweeping the street and the town's residents locked in their homes. On the third night the Murphy forces set fire to McSween's house, which quickly spread to the store. Silhouetted against the flames, the besieged men were forced to make a run for their lives. The Kid escaped, but Alexander McSween went down in a hailstorm of bullets. Altogether, the Three Day Battle resulted in ten killed and nearly twice that number wounded.

Ironically, only days before the showdown, L. G. Murphy had died a natural death in Santa Fe. With their leaders dead, the opposing factions gradually disbanded following the battle. Old animosities still existed, fanned anew when the Kid and his gang turned to rustling as a livelihood. Yet, in the ashes of the McSween store, an official end had been written to the Lincoln County War.

"Life's funny," Garrett concluded. "Nobody hardly remembers McSween and Murphy. But the Kid's still front-page news, and everybody from the governor on down wants to see him hung. Damn queer, the way things turn out."

Inside the saloon, Garrett led the way toward the bar. Then, suddenly reversing himself, he walked to a table where two men were seated. With a wide smile, he beckoned Starbuck over to the table.

"Luke, I'd like you to meet Jack Dobson and Judge Hough. Gents, this here's my new deputy, Luke Starbuck."

Starbuck sensed an instant of hesitation. Jack Dobson, like Chisum, was a survivor of the Lincoln County War. Yet he was politically opposed to the cattleman, and therefore no friend of Pat Garrett's.

After a round of handshakes, Starbuck moved to one side, watchful.

Garrett was in a bragging mood. He informed the men that Starbuck was only one of six new deputies. He went on to state that, with his expanded force, he would soon have the Kid under lock and key. Dobson, a paunchy, whey-faced man, waited until the sheriff paused for breath. Then he smiled, flashing a mouth full of gold-capped teeth, and shook his head.

"What if the Kid don't cooperate, Pat? Six men or sixty, you've still got to catch him."

"Hell's fire!" Garrett beamed. "I got myself some experienced manhunters! Luke and these other boys eat hardcases like the Kid for breakfast. You mark my word, we'll have him in the bag before Christmas!"

"Maybe you will," Dobson chuckled, "maybe you won't. Guess we'll just have to wait and see."

"Whatever the outcome," Judge Hough added quickly, "we wish you luck, Sheriff." He paused, glancing at Starbuck. "And, of course, you too, Deputy."

Starbuck merely nodded. A bloodless man in his late forties, the judge had bleached blue eyes and skin the lifeless texture of parchment. He was tall and rangy, with sallow features and an enigmatic gaze, as though the head of an eagle had been grafted onto the body of a whooping crane.

No one spoke for a moment. Dobson fell silent, while Starbuck and the judge inspected each other.

Then, with heavy good humor, Garrett addressed Judge Hough.

"We'll take all the luck we can get, and I appreciate the sentiment, Judge. Even if you don't mean it, you're a gentleman and a scholar."

With a bluff smile, Garrett turned and walked to the bar. Starbuck joined him, and the barkeep hustled forward with a bottle and glasses. The lawman poured, chuckling softly to himself.

"Bastards!" he grunted. "Sure did my heart good to rub their noses in it."

"I take it Dobson's pulling for the Kid."

"Oh hell, yes!" Garrett hooted. "He'd take sides with the devil himself if he thought it would fix my wagon."

"Seems sort of strange," Starbuck mused aloud. "When you consider the Kid was gunning for him not too long ago."

"Well, like I said, it's a queer world. The Kid used to side with Chisum, and now he rustles Jinglebob cows." He downed his drink, poured another. "Course, where Dobson's concerned, it's a matter of politics. If I don't catch the Kid, then him and his crowd won't have no trouble electin' themselves a sheriff next time around."

"What about the judge?" Starbuck asked. "Where's he fit into it?"

"One of Dobson's cronies," Garrett said without much interest. "His name's Owen Hough. Had himself a pretty fair law practice in Santa Fe at one time. Then Murphy hired him to look after their legal interests, and when the fightin' was over, Dobson got him elected to city judge."

"Seems a little bit like a comedown, doesn't it?"

"Damned if it don't! For my money, he would've been smarter to stick to Santa Fe. Christ, anything beats lickin' Jack Dobson's boots!"

Starbuck had a visceral instinct about such things. He sensed that Judge Owen Hough was no bootlicker. Moreover, he'd noted that Dobson quickly backed off once the judge entered the conversation. It occurred to him that there was more to the alliance of businessman and lawyer than appeared on the surface. But it was a passing thought, and he had no time to explore it further. Garrett's voice intruded with amiable mockery.

"You look like you done started that heavy thinkin' we was talking about."

"Yeah, some," Starbuck allowed. "Only trouble is, we keep adding pieces to the puzzle."

"Maybe so," Garrett commented. "But I get the feelin' you've already fit the first piece into place."

Starbuck nodded. "Suppose you tell me about Fort Sumner."

CHAPTER 5

A hunter's moon slipped out from behind the clouds. The landscape around Fort Sumner, blanketed by a light snowfall, was momentarily limned in an ice-blue brilliance. Then the moon faded, and a dull overcast once more bathed the settlement in darkness.

Starbuck and John Poe stood outside an adobe at the edge of the settlement. The building, like many of those at Fort Sumner, was deserted. But it commanded a view of the road leading west, toward the Jicarilla Mountains. For the past two nights, the adobe had served as a hideout for the lawmen and their horses. With no fires allowed, the thick walls also provided shelter from the bitter cold. Bedded down inside were Pat Garrett and his regular deputies, Jim Bell and Bob Ollinger. The four new deputies, Starbuck's men, completed the posse.

Starbuck was playing a hunch. From past experience, he'd learned there was a pattern to any manhunt. Outlaws who had evaded capture for any length of time often grew bold, and careless. The leader of a gang, after several successful jobs, inevitably developed an inflated opinion of himself. A by-product of that vanity was an ever-increasing contempt for lawmen. With time, simple audacity gave way to recklessness, and caution ceased to be a factor. Almost without exception, the leader of an outlaw band assumed a mantle of invincibility, and godlike arrogance.

All he'd learned to date convinced Starbuck that Billy the Kid had fallen into a similar pattern. Little known by his real name, William Bonney, the Kid had thumbed his nose at the law since age fifteen. Barely twenty-one now, he had killed eight men in the last six years, and never once come close to facing the hangman's rope. His exploits had brought him the adulation of the common people and the respect of a gang of ruffians feared throughout the territory. It was heady stuff, quite enough to turn any man cocksure and overly bold.

The information Starbuck had gleaned from Pat Garrett merely confirmed his hunch. The Kid alternated raids on Chisum's Jinglebob with forays into the Panhandle. While there was no set timetable to the raids, there was nonetheless a definite pattern. The Kid always struck each location once a month, and he *never* struck the same spot twice in a row. Which led to a very tempting conclusion.

The gang's aborted raid on the LX had occurred precisely two weeks past. Only three nights ago the Jinglebob had lost more than a hundred head to rustlers. Logic dictated that it was the Kid's handiwork, and it might be deduced that the gang would again skirt the Jicarilla Mountains on a gradual eastward swing to the Panhandle. Starbuck was convinced the eastward swing regularly included a layover at Fort Sumner.

An abandoned army post, Fort Sumner was remote and starkly uninviting. Pete Maxwell, one of the few ranchers in the area, had taken over several of the buildings as headquarters for his cattle operation. A small settlement had evolved, with a general store and the saloon previously owned by Pat Garrett. Most of the residents were Mexican vaqueros and their families, and the local economy revolved around Maxwell's ranch. The nearest law was in Lincoln, ninety miles southwest, and native-born Mexicans had small regard for gringo peace officers. As a result, the Kid was free to come and go as he pleased. He was widely admired—polite to the women and generous to the men who drank with him—and always welcome at Fort Sumner. No one there, Pete Maxwell included, would think of betraying him.

For two days and a night the lawmen had remained hidden in the adobe. The road was a narrow track, seldom used, and no one from the settlement had as yet discovered them. But now, early on the second night, Starbuck's concern was deepening. With no fire, and the men limited to cold rations, the chance of a storm posed serious problems. Even though the snowfall was still light, he questioned the wisdom of staying too much longer. At last, after searching the overcast sky, he turned to Poe.

"I'm thinking we'll have to call it quits."

"That wouldn't bother Garrett's boys none."

"Yeah, they're not much, are they?"

"Couple of peckerheads, if you ask me."

John Poe was a methodical man, stingy with words, but a dead shot and absolutely fearless in a fight. Somewhere in his late thirties, he was powerfully built, with ruddy features and an inscrutable manner. Aside from Ben Langham, he was the only man Starbuck had ever fully trusted.

"Suppose we stick it out till midnight." Starbuck paused, studying the clouds a moment. "If it hasn't cleared by then, we'll let the boys build a fire and cook some hot grub."

"Whatever you say."

"You got a better idea?"

Poe rolled his quid to the other jaw and spat a stream of tobacco juice. "Not unless you've got a bearskin coat handy."

"No such luck—"

Starbuck suddenly stopped. He peered through the swirling snow, listening. Then he heard it again, the faint jingle of saddle gear somewhere in the distance. He whirled to Poe.

"Quick, inside! Get the boys ready!"

While Poe awakened the men, Starbuck stationed himself at the window nearest the road. Within the space of a minute, Garrett was crouched beside the doorway, and the deputies were positioned by the windows fronting the adobe. No one spoke, listening intently as the sound of hoofbeats drew closer.

Then, one at a time, five riders materialized out of the snow. They were strung out in single file, their horses held to a walk. Hunched deep within their coats, the men were dim shapes, their features indistinguishable.

The riders were within yards of the adobe when Pat Garrett abruptly stepped through the doorway. He raised his hand, rapped out an order. *"Halt!"*

The lead rider jerked erect, clawing his coat aside. There was a gleam of metal as his gun cleared leather, then Starbuck shot him. He screamed, pitching sideways out of the saddle, and tumbled to the ground. Before Starbuck could lever another round into his carbine, the other riders reined sharply around and gigged their horses into a gallop. The remaining lawmen at last opened fire, but it was too late. The drifting snow closed in behind the riders, and an instant later the thud of hoofbeats faded away to silence.

Starbuck moved to the door, brushing past Garrett, and walked to the fallen rider. Garrett hesitated a moment, then the deputies crowded through the doorway, and they trooped along in a bunch behind Starbuck. As they crowded around, he struck a match, cupping it with his hands over the dead man's face.

"Anybody know him?"

"Tom O'Folliard," Garrett mumbled. "He's one of the Kid's men."

"So we had him," Starbuck rose, his voice edged, "and let him get away."

"Sorry." Garrett ducked his head. "I thought maybe they'd come along without a fight."

"Well, Sheriff, you damn near got your ass shot off! Of all the fool stunts—"

Starbuck turned away, furious. He stalked toward the adobe, staring straight ahead. At the doorway, he suddenly spun around, motioning to the deputies.

"Get saddled!" he ordered. "Poe, take a couple of men and go round up some lanterns."

"That's crazy!" Garrett protested. "We'll lose their tracks in the snow."

"We ride in ten minutes."

Starbuck turned and entered the adobe.

The trail twisted and dodged for a week. The Kid crossed mountain ranges and mesas, doubled back and circled, attempting every trick known to lose his pursuers. But the foul weather held and the skies remained overcast; for all his cunning, there was no way to erase horse tracks in fresh snow. The posse was never more than a few hours behind.

Starbuck drove the men with dogged relentlessness. The bitter cold sapped their spirits, and the chase, punishing to man and animal alike, slowly drained their vitality. By the sixth day, they were haggard and bleary-eyed with fatigue. Their grumbling had turned to surly ill-temper, and the slightest offense provoked an argument. Yet the men, despite their rebellious mood, were the least of Starbuck's worries. Their horses were spent, slogging heavy-footed through the snow, and their rations were running low. Without fresh mounts and adequate provisions, they were finished. Unless the Kid was caught quickly, he would not be caught at all.

Camp was pitched that evening on the windswept banks of a small creek. Supper consisted of boiled jerky and hardtack, washed down with coffee. Sitting off to one side, Starbuck pondered their situation, and found the prospects bleak. His one consolation was that the Kid faced an equally miserable predicament. Pressed hard, never allowed to pause or replenish their supplies, the gang would also be on short rations tonight. He took bitter comfort from the thought.

Starbuck drained the last of his coffee, and rose. He walked to the fire, where Garrett squatted with his hands held to the flames. Tossing his cup on the ground, Starbuck caught the lawman's eyes and nodded. Turning, he moved a short distance downstream, and Garrett joined him a moment later.

"I hate to admit it," Starbuck commenced in a sandy voice, "but we've about run out our string."

"No argument there," Garrett said bluntly. "Even good men can only be pushed so far."

"The hell of it is," Starbuck frowned, "I figure the Kid's only a couple of hours ahead of us. Galls me to quit when we're that close."

"We've got no choice," Garrett reminded him. "It'd take us another day to close the gap, and by then we'd be afoot. Horses got their limits, too."

Garrett's tone was waspish, disgruntled. Though he was nominally in command, even his own deputies understood that it was Starbuck who gave the orders. The arrangement grated on him, and day by day his mood had sharpened. Yet he needed Starbuck, and for all his simmering resentment, he continued to swallow his pride. The Kid was his ticket to bigger things.

Starbuck gave him a speculative look. "What's up ahead, the direction the Kid took?"

"Lots of open space."

"No towns, no ranches? Nothing?"

"Oh, there's an old shepherd's hut at Stinking Springs, but nothin' else within a day's ride. It's pretty sparse over this way, mostly sheep country."

"A shepherd's hut," Starbuck said slowly. "How far off?"

"Maybe—" Garrett stopped, eyes suddenly alert. "A couple of hours, three at the outside."

"You think the Kid—"

"Damn right he would!" Garrett interrupted. "He knows this country like he knows the back of his hand."

"That being the case, it makes sense he'd camp there to get out of the weather."

"Course it does! With dark comin' on, it'd be the most natural thing on earth."

"Suppose we let the horses rest till midnight. You reckon we could take it easy and still make it there by sunup?"

"Why, hell, yes! Even if we had to walk 'em

partway, we'd get there with time to spare."

Starbuck let the idea percolate a few moments. "It's a gamble, but we might just catch the Kid with his drawers down. You game?"

"I'm game." Garrett glanced toward the fire. "I don't know about the men."

"Well, Pat, if they're not, then we'll just handle it ourselves. How's that sound?"

"By God, you got yourself a deal."

The men heard them out. The idea of a night march brought some low grumbling, but no one seriously objected. Instead, like a lodestone freshly glimpsed, their thoughts turned to Stinking Springs, and the Kid.

By dawn, crouched low in an arroyo, the men were in position. The stone hut, located on a desolate stretch of prairie, had no windows and only one door. The gang's horses were picketed in front of the hut, and shortly before sunup, a tendril of smoke drifted from the stovepipe chimney.

A few minutes later, one of the outlaws stepped outside and began unbuttoning his fly. Without warning, Garrett fired, followed instantly by shots from three of the deputies. The outlaw reeled backwards, clutching his chest, and staggered through the doorway. From inside the hut there was a loud commotion, men shouting and cursing. Then a shrill voice, rising to a maddened pitch, drowned out the others.

"They've murdered you, Charlie! Kill some of the sonsabitches before you die!"

"That's the Kid," Garrett said quickly. "Watch 'em now!"

The wounded outlaw lurched through the door. The lawmen watched in disbelief as he hobbled toward them. His shirtfront was drenched with blood and he held a cocked pistol in his hand. Yet no one spoke, and without command, they held their fire. Some twenty yards away, the outlaw stumbled to a halt and his mouth opened. The words were lost in a gush of blood and his eyes rolled back in his head. He fell face down in the snow.

Starbuck raised his carbine, sighting carefully. He shot the horse nearest the door, and grunted with satisfaction as the animal went down, blocking the entrance. He worked the lever and placed three rapid shots at the base of the stovepipe. A fourth shot sent it flying off the roof, and within moments smoke began seeping through cracks in the door. He smiled, lowering the carbine, and turned to Garrett.

"Talk to the Kid. Tell him the show's over."

Garrett nodded, cupped his hands to his mouth. "Hey, Kid! It's me, Pat Garrett! Can you hear me?"

"I hear you, Pat. What's on your mind?"

"Gettin' a little smoky in there, is it?"

"Not bad. Whyn't you come on down and get a snootful?"

"You're boxed in, Kid! Nowhere to go! Call it quits!"

"Like hell! We'll just sit tight and let you freeze your balls off out there."

Starbuck whispered something to Garrett, and the lawman bobbed his head. "Won't work, Kid!" Garrett shouted. "You try waitin' till dark and we'll just kill your horses. Even if you bust out of that hut, you'd never make it on foot. Wise up and toss in your hand!"

Silence descended on the hut. Smoke continued to filter through the door, and gradually the sound of men coughing became louder. After several minutes the Kid's voice suddenly broke the stillness.

"You win, Pat! We've had enough!"

"No funny business!" Garrett yelled. "Shuck your gunbelts! Come out with your hands in the air!"

A few moments passed, then the door creaked open. One by one, dimly obscured by the smoke, the outlaws walked from the hut. At Starbuck's suggestion, Garrett ordered them to move forward, away from the picketed horses. The men complied, halting on his command, their arms raised.

With the deputies covering them, Garrett and Starbuck scrambled from the arroyo. Their carbines held at hip level, they separated and moved to within a few yards of the outlaws. Starbuck had no trouble identifying the Kid. He was runt-sized, with a lantern jaw and the look of a bantam gamecock. His eyes were the color of carpenter's chalk, and cold. He waited until they halted, then gave Garrett a lopsided grin.

"Don't shoot, Pat. We'll come peaceable."

"Cut the wisecracks," Garrett growled. "There's nothin' funny about where you're headed."

"Yeah, well, it ain't all that serious either. I've slipped away from some real lawmen, Pat. I don't guess you'll gimme too much trouble."

"Don't get me riled, Billy! I mean it now!"

"Wouldn't think of it, Pat." The Kid laughed, and his gaze shifted to Starbuck. "You the jasper that did the fancy shootin'?"

Starbuck regarded him without expression. "What makes you ask?"

"Just curious."

"You try to make a break," Garrett cut in, "and he'll sure enough show you some fancy shootin'."

"He'd have to do it," the Kid grinned. "You couldn't've hit that stovepipe if it was jammed straight up your butthole."

"By God, that's it!"

Garrett ordered one of his deputies to fetch the manacles from his saddlebags. Ten minutes later they had the outlaws mounted and were ready to move out. With Garrett in the lead, and Starbuck riding shotgun, they turned their horses toward Santa Fe.

CHAPTER 6

Three days before New Year's, Starbuck crossed the plaza and walked toward the territorial jail. Until a trial date could be set, the Kid and his gang were being held there for safekeeping. Only then, according to Garrett, would they be transported back to Lincoln.

Starbuck now had reason to believe otherwise.

The plaza swarmed with activity. A town built on commerce and politics, the territorial capital was once the terminus for the Santa Fe Trail. Winter was the slow season, but as a major trade center, Santa Fe was never really idle. Exchange between Mexico and the United States was its principal business, and tons of trade goods, arriving now by train rather than wagon caravan, were stored there year round. Shops around the square were crowded, and open-air markets on the plaza itself were thronged with people. The holidays had done nothing to slow the brisk pace of trade.

To Starbuck, all the clamor and hubbub was a vast annoyance. He felt nothing of the festive spirit, and the season of brotherly love seemed to him an ironic joke. His thoughts were on deception and double-dealing. And as he moved through the crowds, he was plagued by a sense of betrayal.

Arriving in Santa Fe the day after Christmas, he had been filled with quiet elation. Ben Langham's killer had been caught, and he'd completed the job in slightly less than three weeks. The fact that Garrett got credit for capturing the Kid—and evidenced no intention of sharing the limelight—bothered him not at all. The Kid had been charged with an old murder, the assassination of a Lincoln County sheriff some two years past. It was a strong case, with several eyewitnesses, and there was no question the Kid would be tried and hung. Though impatient to see the Kid mount the scaffold, Starbuck was satisfied with the arrangement. An eye for an eye would shortly be exacted.

Then, unwittingly, one of Garrett's deputies had talked out of turn. Night before last, with several drinks under his belt, Bob Ollinger let slip that the Kid had been offered a deal. Questioned by Starbuck, the deputy refused to elaborate. But he drunkenly implied the Kid could escape hanging by turning state's evidence against those behind the rustling. His last statement, though somewhat cryptic, was the most telling.

"The Kid spilled his guts before and he'll do it again."

Starbuck braced Garrett later that night and demanded an explanation. The lawman professed ignorance, claiming Ollinger was a blowhard and given to an overactive imagination when drunk. Pressed for details, he did admit that Chisum believed there was a mastermind behind the rustling. He declined to speculate, however, on whether Chisum would go so far as to offer the Kid a deal. Nor would he discuss the motives, personal or otherwise, that might prompt the cattleman to do so.

Unconvinced, Starbuck began an investigation of his own early next morning. Having failed with Garrett, he resolved to trick the Kid into an admission. But that would require a bold hand, and sufficient facts to give his bluff the ring of truth. He needed information about the last time the Kid had "spilled his guts," and his search began in the territorial records of the Lincoln County War. By late afternoon, the trail led to the former Attorney General of New Mexico. There, employing a discreet form of interrogation, he uncovered the full story.

Following the Three Day Battle in Lincoln, Governor Lew Wallace issued a general amnesty for all offenses committed during the "war." Some months later, a lawyer who had supported Alexander McSween was callously murdered by two former members of the Murphy—Dobson faction. Upon learning the Kid had witnessed the shooting, Governor Wallace promised immunity, and a full pardon, if he would testify. The Kid agreed, submitting to arrest, and gave testimony before a grand jury. Then, for no apparent reason, he escaped from jail and promptly returned to cattle rustling. The governor publicly denounced him and withdrew all forms of immunity. Since that time, flaunting the law, the Kid had grown even more vicious. He was known to have murdered three men in cold blood, including an unarmed Indian Agent on the Mescalero reservation. Why he'd broken his agreement with the governor, however, remained a mystery. One of the many surrounding Billy the Kid.

Late last night, reflecting on what he'd learned, Starbuck had found sleep impossible. He tossed and turned, trying to formulate a plan, and hadn't closed his eyes until shortly before dawn. But now, crossing the plaza, his confidence was restored. The answer had come to him at breakfast this morning, and it had come with startling clarity.

The Kid, like all outlaws, viewed any peace officer with suspicion and distrust. The trick was simply to make him believe he was being tricked.

Starbuck had no compunction about using subterfuge and guile. Experience had taught him that a certain breed of outlaw had no concept of morality. For reasons he failed to understand, the public made folk heroes of such men as Jesse James and Sam Bass. And Billy the Kid. Cast in the role of the underdog, these men were thought to have compassion for the downtrodden and an inborn hatred of injustice. But such attributes were the invention of dime novels, and the public's bizarre need to create legends larger than life. Four years as a range detective had convinced Starbuck that these mankillers lacked even the most fundamental code of decency. Only a fool dealt with them on the basis of fair play, and only by being utterly pragmatic had he survived their treachery and malice.

Contrary to popular belief, he knew the Kid was nothing more than a common murderer. Far from a gunfighter, the young outlaw had given none of his victims an even break. Of the eight men he'd killed, at least seven had been gunned down with no chance to defend themselves. Folklore and truth, where the Kid was concerned, had absolutely nothing in common.

To Starbuck, there was more than passing similarity to a rabid animal. If a mad dog was terrorizing the countryside, no one would hesitate to shoot it down on sight. The Kid was no different. And Starbuck now regretted that the Kid had allowed himself to be taken prisoner. Justice would have been more swiftly served if the young outlaw had chosen to make a fight of it. Starbuck would have then killed him quickly and efficiently, thereby ridding the world of one more mad dog. Yet the Kid still lived, and, given the chance he might elude the hangman's rope, Starbuck saw no alternative. He somehow had to trick the Kid into rendering his own death warrant.

Starbuck was admitted to the territorial jail without question. As one of Garrett's deputies, it was only natural that he would drop around to check on the star prisoner. The cell block was large, with a wide corridor, and he was relieved to see that the Kid had been segregated from the rest of the gang.

What he had in mind would work better without an audience.

Locked in adjoining cells, Dave Rudabaugh, Tom Pickett, and Bill Wilson watched passively as the guard led Starbuck down the corridor. Toward the rear, all the cells were empty; there were no prisoners on either side of the Kid or across the corridor. He lay sprawled on a rickety bunk, staring at the ceiling.

The guard halted before the door. "Look alive, Kid. You got yourself a visitor." Turning, he nodded to Starbuck. "Give a yell if you need anything."

"Much obliged."

Starbuck waited until he was out of earshot, then moved closer to the cell door. "Mornin', Billy. Thought I'd come by and see how they're treating you."

"No complaint."

"How's the food?"

"Tolerable."

"Glad to hear it." Starbuck pulled out the makings and began rolling a cigarette. "Care for a smoke?"

"Don't mind if I do."

The Kid rose from his bunk in one motion and stepped to the door. Starbuck passed the makings through the bars, and smiled. "Keep it, if you want. I can always get more."

"Thanks."

After the Kid had built himself a cigarette, Starbuck struck a match. They both lit up and stood smoking a moment in silence. Then the Kid regarded him with a crooked grin.

"You through dancin' around the Maypole?"

"Come again?"

"Whatever it is, whyn't you just get to it? You ain't here to shoot the breeze and we both know it."

Starbuck had seen his share of hardcases. In Texas, and elsewhere he'd ridden, there was no scarcity of the breed. The young outlaw was cast from a similar mold, and yet, there was something different about him. The pale blue eyes were steady and confident, and behind the gaze was a cocksure certainty more menacing than a bald-faced threat. The Kid was one of those oddities of God's handiwork, a man purged of conscience. He could kill with the icy detachment of an executioner, and never suffer a moment's remorse. If Starbuck had needed any justification, he found it staring at him through the bars. He decided it was time to trim the Kid's wick.

"I've got a message from a mutual friend."

"Yeah, who's that?"

"No names." Starbuck glanced over his shoulder. "Some of these places, the walls have got ears."

"So what's the message?"

"He says time's running out. If you figure to make a deal, you better do it pretty quick."

"Christ, the old bastard only contacted me day before yesterday. What's the rush?"

Starbuck had one of the answers needed, and it enabled him to proceed with greater assurance. He shrugged. "You might recall, he gives orders, not explanations. Hell, I don't even know who it was that contacted you! But the old man evidently thought the message wasn't strong enough. He sent word for me to have a talk with you."

"Tell him to get the ants out of his pants. I still got time to think it over."

"Not if they set an early trial date, you don't."

"Come off it," the Kid scoffed. "What's that got to do with anything?"

"Plenty," Starbuck said earnestly. "Once you're remanded to the Lincoln court, there'll be lots more pressure for the governor to keep hands off."

The Kid gave him a swift, sidelong look. "Who you tryin' to shit, Starbuck?"

"I don't follow you."

"In a pig's ass! You think I don't know who you are?"

Starbuck almost smiled. He cautioned himself to go slow, allow the Kid to swallow the hook on his own. "Suppose you tell me who I am."

"You're a goddamn range detective! You draw your pay from the Panhandle Cattlemen's Association!"

"That's not exactly a secret."

"Aww for Chrissake!" The Kid laughed suddenly, a harsh sound in the cramped cell. "Are you gonna stand there and tell me you're not tryin' to run a sandy?"

"Whoa, now!" Starbuck looked genuinely puzzled. "You just lost me going around the turn."

"Horseshit! You come to the territory to see me planted, and there ain't no two ways about it. You must think I'm some kind of fool to believe you'd take a hand in anything that would stop me from gettin' hung."

"You're talking about Langham—the fellow that was killed over in the Panhandle—aren't you?"

"Don't try puttin' words in my mouth. I'm saying you want me dead, and the reason don't matter."

"You're wrong," Starbuck insisted. "The Association wants the rustling stopped, and that's their only interest. The way they figure it, Langham's dead and gone, and there's not a helluva lot of profit in vengeance."

"Profit?" the Kid said scornfully. "What the devil's profit got to do with it?"

"Everything," Starbuck nodded gravely. "You know it yourself: the only thing that matters to the big boys is how much dinero they put in the bank. They're willing to trade you in order to get a shot at the head dog behind all this rustling."

"You're lying! I can smell it like you'd been dunked in sheep dip."

"Why would I lie? I've got no reason."

"I don't know," the Kid said doubtfully. "But I still say it stinks."

"Then you'd better take off the blinders and start thinking straight. Unless the Panhandle crowd was in agreement with—the old man—how would I even know you'd been offered a deal? I'm strictly a messenger boy, just following orders. That's all there is to it, plain and simple."

The Kid turned away. He was obviously confused and suspicious, not at all convinced he'd heard the truth. He took a long pull on his cigarette, staring at a spot of sunlight on the floor. Finally, with a look of sudden resolve, he glanced around at Starbuck.

"No soap," he said shortly. "Tell the old man I pass."

"Hold off—"

"Like hell! I got sold down the river once before, and I ain't gonna fall for it again."

"You mean a couple of years ago, when the governor got you to testify before the grand jury?"

"Damn right!" The Kid spoke in an aggrieved tone. "The sonovabitch spoon-fed me a bunch of promises, and after I delivered, he went ahead and pressed charges against me anyway."

"You're plumb certain about that, are you?"

"If I wasn't, why the hell would I've broke jail?"

"Well—" Starbuck hesitated, seemingly at a loss. "I suppose you've got a point, but of course that time around you were playing a lone hand. This time, there are some important people who'll bring pressure to bear on the governor. Believe me—with what's at stake—they won't sell you out."

"I don't trust none of 'em," the Kid said stubbornly. "Once I testified, they'd welch on the deal faster'n scat! So you just tell 'em I said to jam it up their butt."

Starbuck felt a surge of triumph. He set his features in a downcast expression, but inside he knew he had soured the Kid on any sort of deal. The trial would go forward, and all in due time, Ben Langham's killer would be hung. He was on the verge of letting it rest there, but on impulse, he suddenly changed his mind. Perhaps it was possible to dust two birds with a single stone. One last trick.

"You know," he suggested casually, "it wouldn't hurt your chances none to hedge your bet. Even if you mean to hold out, you could still play both ends against the middle."

"I don't savvy," the Kid said woodenly. "Hedge my bet how?"

"Give the old man a nibble, show your good faith. Name a few names."

"You're nuttier'n a fruitcake!"

"Wait a minute," Starbuck stilled his outburst with upraised palms. "I didn't say anything about testifying. You wouldn't even have to give a deposition. But if you named some names—and it turned out to be the straight goods—then it would sure leave the door open."

"Yeah, but I wouldn't have nothin' left to sell either."

"No, you're wrong," Starbuck told him. "Without your testimony, it's all hearsay, isn't it? So any way you cut it, you'll still improve your hand."

The Kid paused, as though weighing his words. After a marked silence, he dropped his cigarette on the floor, ground it out underfoot. Then he looked up.

"Joe Coghlin. Coghlin's Slaughterhouse in Lincoln."

"Are you saying he's the top dog?"

"No," the Kid stalled. "But he's the one that buys the rustled stock."

"Who calls the shots?" Starbuck pressed. "It's no good unless I've got the whole story."

"Well, let's just say Coghlin don't hardly take a leak till he checks with Jack Dobson."

"That's all?"

"All you're gonna get."

It was enough. Starbuck left the jail whistling to himself. Once outside, his thoughts turned to the Jinglebob and John Chisum. And he began planning the next step.

CHAPTER 7

The morning stage pulled into Santa Fe an hour late. The driver brought his team to a halt before the express office and set the brake lever with a hard kick. As the agent hurried outside, a band of street urchins gathered around. He waded through them, cursing their ancestry in broken Spanish, and hustled forward to open the coach door.

Judge Owen Hough was the first passenger to alight from the coach. Dusting himself off, he moved into the shade of the office portico. There he waited impatiently while the luggage was unloaded from the rear boot. After claiming his bag, he gave one of the Mexican *golfillos* a dollar to run it over to the hotel. Brushing the other children aside, he turned and walked quickly toward the east side of the plaza.

At the corner, Judge Hough slowed his pace. He took a cigar from inside his coat, snipping the end with one clean bite, and pretended to search his pockets for a match. While he lit the cigar, his eyes roamed the plaza, scanning the crowds for a familiar face. Satisfied he hadn't been seen, he snuffed the match and rounded the corner onto a side street. Ahead were several stores and warehouses, framed against a backdrop of the Sangre de Cristo Mountains. He strode to an alleyway separating a feed store and a livery stable, and carefully inspected the street in both directions. Then he turned into the alley.

Walking to the rear of the feed store, he mounted a short flight of stairs. He paused before a back door, rapping lightly with his knuckles, and entered. The room was windowless and sparsely furnished, empty except for two chairs and a wooden table. On the table was a kerosene lamp, the wick turned low. A large man, his features shadowed by the dim light, rose from one of the chairs. He seemed strangely out of place in the drab surroundings. His gray mustache was neatly trimmed and waxed, and he wore a frock coat and a stiff winged collar covered by a black cravat. His pearl stickpin gleamed in the umber lampglow.

He smiled and extended his hand. "Good to see you, Owen. I was beginning to think you wouldn't make it."

"The stage was late." Hough shook hands, tossing his hat on the table. "A rockslide outside Blue Springs held us up almost an hour."

"I assume you took the usual precautions?"

"Of course."

Once every month Owen Hough traveled to Santa Fe. On the pretext of personal business affairs, his trips seemed perfectly routine and aroused

72

little interest in Lincoln. Only Jack Dobson knew the true nature of his business, and no one knew that his monthly reports were delivered in the dingy back room of a feed store. As a further precaution, the meetings were always held on random dates, selected a month in advance by the man who received his report. There was no correspondence between them, and no record existed of the meetings ever having taken place. Upon arriving in Santa Fe, it was Hough's responsibility to enter the back-alley storeroom without being observed. The penalty for failure, though never articulated by either man, was mutually understood.

"Well, let's get to it, shall we?"

Hough nodded, taking a chair across from the other man. He puffed on his cigar, waiting, aware that a certain protocol dictated how the meeting was to proceed. A moment passed, then the large man thoughtfully twisted one end of his mustache.

"Our meeting was well timed this month. The capture of Mr. Bonney and his cutthroats presents us with a delicate situation. One, I hasten to add, that has intriguing possibilities."

"Oh?" Hough said cautiously. "Such as?"

"We'll come to that later. For the moment, suppose you brief me on the state of things in Lincoln."

"There's been no great change. Chisum's health continues to deteriorate, but not alarmingly. He's just dying slowly, by degrees."

"Has his doctor visited the ranch?"

"Not to my knowledge."

"Are you saying you're not certain?"

"I'll rephrase it—no—the doctor has not visited him."

"Then we must surmise his condition remains unchanged."

"As a matter of fact," Hough replied, "our latest information has it that his spirits have improved somewhat. Apparently the Kid's capture gave him a boost, mentally if not physically."

"I see that as no consequence. In the long term, a momentary lift in spirits alters nothing."

"Perhaps not, at least where Chisum is concerned. But it's had a marked effect on our own situation."

"Would you care to be more specific?"

"Our associates have come down with a case of nerves."

"Dobson?"

"And Coghlin," Hough added. "They're frightened out of their wits the Kid will start talking."

"About the rustling operation?"

"Yes, primarily that. You see, Coghlin has dealt directly with the Kid on several occasions. And through him, that establishes an indirect link to Dobson. They don't trust the Kid and they don't trust each other—and despite all my assurances, it's evolved into a matter of fear feeding on fear."

"But that's ridiculous! The Kid has been charged with murder, not rustling."

"True enough. Of course, as Coghlin put it, the

Kid would weasel on his own mother to save himself."

"In other words, he might implicate them in exchange for a lesser charge. Or at the very worst, a commutation in the event he's sentenced to hang. Is that it?"

"Exactly."

"And you personally, Owen? Are you worried as well?"

"No, of course not," Hough said without conviction. "My hands are clean. So far as anyone knows, I'm just another political hack, a nobody."

"On the contrary. I detect a note in your voice, some slight apprehension. Are you perhaps concerned that the link tying Coghlin to Dobson extends equally to you?"

"You're mistaken, Warren. I have no reservations whatever. Absolutely none."

"Let us hope so. Conspiracy is a nasty charge, and as we both know, you are the only link connecting our associates here in Santa Fe to the affairs in Lincoln. They might well become nervous themselves if it was felt you were no longer reliable."

"I understand. And I assure you, Warren, there's no need for concern."

"But if there were"—a querulous squint—"let me be blunt. You were sent to Lincoln to do a job. Dobson and Coghlin are your responsibility, Owen. We depend on you to hold them in line, and see to it that they perform as directed. Any display of weakness on their part reflects adversely on your leadership. So, as the saying goes, a word to the wise. When you return to Lincoln, correct the situation immediately. Agreed?"

"Agreed," Hough repeated in a low voice. "Of course, it would help if I could return with something a bit more substantial regarding the Kid."

"Then you may inform our friends that Mr. Bonney will not talk."

"He won't?"

"You have my word on it."

"How can you be sure?"

"In exchange for his silence, Mr. Bonney will be offered a change of venue. Naturally, it won't make the slightest bit of difference in the verdict. But he'll be led to believe, through his defense attorney, that a change of venue represents his one hope. Like the proverbial drowning man, he will grasp at the idea of a trial anywhere other than Lincoln. The arrangements were concluded only this morning with the district judge, and Mr. Bonney will be so informed this afternoon. Do you approve?"

"It's—Warren, it's damn near Machiavellian!"

"Why, thank you, Owen. I consider that a rare compliment."

Owen Hough, by virtue of arrangements with unscrupulous men, had prospered greatly. Once a man of principle, his convictions had long ago been eroded by the practice of compromise. Slowly, trading his beliefs for position and material gain, he had become enmeshed in a web of obligations so unconscionable that he lost sight of conventional morality. Today, no less corrupt than the man across from him, he thought it a masterful stroke that the Kid would be duped into silence.

"One thing, though," he said at length. "A moment ago, you said the change of venue won't affect the verdict. I take it you mean the Kid will hang, regardless?"

"Yes, that's correct. Not only has he become a liability, but his execution will serve to distract Chisum. As we've discussed before, Chisum very likely suspects there is more to it than the rustling. With Bonney dead, however, those suspicions will be dampened considerably."

"On the other hand," Hough said hesitantly, "Chisum might look upon this as an opportunity. With the Stockgrowers' Association behind him, he could bring pressure to bear on the governor. Then, once the Kid's been sentenced to death, he could offer commutation in return for information. At that point, the Kid wouldn't hesitate to talk."

"There will be no commutation, Owen. I guarantee it! You just leave the governor to us, and go on about business as normal."

"You're saying, even if Chisum makes the offer there's no way he can deliver. So as a result, the Kid won't talk."

"Precisely."

Hough took a deep breath, blew it out heavily. "What about this fellow Starbuck? He has a reputation as a real bulldog. If Chisum hires him to dig deeper, he might just uncover something we've overlooked."

"Your Mr. Starbuck represents one of the intriguing possibilities I mentioned earlier."

"In what way?"

"As you say, he's an experienced detective. Because of that, Chisum will respect his opinion. We have only to convince Starbuck it's a simple case of rustling—nothing to do with politics—and he in turn will convince Chisum."

"How do we accomplish that?"

"Quite simple. We allow the rustling operation to die with William Bonney. In any event, it has already served its purpose: namely, to speed Chisum to his grave. So we let the rustling stop here, and everyone walks away believing it was the work of one man. Or in this case . . . a kid . . . Billy the Kid."

"I don't know." Hough sounded uncertain. "Maybe it's too simple. From what I've heard about Starbuck, he's not the type to be taken in easily."

"You correct me if I'm wrong, Owen. We've established that Bonney will not talk, regardless of the circumstances."

"Yes."

"The rustling operation has ended, and with Bonney's silence, there's no way to trace it to either Dobson or Coghlin."

"That's right."

"And aside from some unfounded suspicions,

Chisum has no way of connecting any of this to the political situation."

"Yes, that's correct, also."

"So there you have it. We've anticipated every contingency."

Hough made a small nod of acknowledgment. "Yes, it appears you have."

"Then I suggest you return to Lincoln and put our affairs in order. I needn't remind you that the Pecos Valley is all that lies between us and absolute control of the territory. We depend on you to have all the machinery in place the day John Chisum dies."

"I won't let you down, Warren."

"We never thought otherwise, Owen. Now, if, there's nothing else, suppose we depart in the usual manner. I'll see you here the twelfth of next month."

Owen Hough unfolded from the chair, tugged his coat smooth. He shook hands, not at all warmed by the other man's smile. Then he moved to the door and stepped outside. The winter air chilled the sheen of perspiration on his forehead.

Starbuck spotted him leaving the alley. On his way back to the hotel, he had paused to admire a centerfire rig in the window of a saddlemaker. As he turned to cross the plaza, he saw Hough emerge onto the side street. He quickly ducked inside the saddle shop.

Watching through the flyblown window, he sensed his instincts hadn't played him false. Not ten minutes ago the Kid had mentioned two names, Joe Coghlin and Jack Dobson. Now, by some quirk that beggared coincidence, the political crony of one of those men appeared in Santa Fe. There were, he told himself, perhaps a dozen explanations for the judge's presence in Santa Fe. Yet in the same instant he knew there was no reasonable explanation for what he'd just seen. Owen Hough was not the type to be skulking around in the alleyway of a feed store.

The judge turned the corner and walked west along the plaza. Starbuck waited until he had mingled with the crowd, then moved through the door of the saddle shop. He was torn between trailing Hough and investigating the feed store. But the debate lasted only a moment. He decided the feed store could await another time.

As he started across the plaza, he caught movement out of the corner of his eye. Something made him look around, his gaze directed to the side street, and he froze. A man emerged from the same alleyway, acting altogether too casual. From his dress, frock coat and striped trousers, he had no more business in a feed store than the judge. He walked briskly to the corner, looking straight ahead, and crossed to the south side of the plaza.

Starbuck followed him. The decision to do so was visceral, too compelling to ignore. Some gut instinct told him the man with the waxed mustache had, only moments before, parted company with Owen Hough. Their meeting, quite obviously, had been held in secret. And it was clear that they had left the feed store separately to avoid being seen together. All of which indicated they had something to hide. Something that might—or might not—have bearing on the rustling operation in Lincoln. But very definitely something that had to be explored further.

Hanging back in the crowd, Starbuck trailed the man to the Mercantile National Bank. There, turning into a stairwell, the man ascended to the second floor. Cautious now, Starbuck climbed the stairs without haste, listening as footsteps faded along a central corridor. He timed it perfectly, topping the upper landing in time to see the frock coat disappear through a door at the end of the hall. He walked down the passageway only far enough to inspect the door. The top half was frosted glass, and the word PRIVATE had been inscribed in gilt letters. His gaze swung to the adjoining door, which appeared to be the entrance to a suite of offices. He studied the legend painted there.

THE SANTA FE LAND & DEVELOPMENT CO.
WARREN F. MITCHELL
PRESIDENT

Starbuck turned and retraced his steps along the corridor. Outside the bank, he paused and rolled a smoke, pondering the strange turn of events. There were no answers, only hard questions, but one thing was clear.

His next stop was the Jinglebob, and a talk with John Chisum.

CHAPTER 8

Starbuck rode into the Jinglebob on New Year's Day. At the door, he was again met by Sallie Chisum. Her greeting was pleasant and seemingly guileless; but he wondered how much she knew of her father's affairs. By now, he had learned that her mother was dead, and despite her youth, she had assumed the duties of mistress of the house. He thought it likely that she knew a good deal more than she pretended.

John Chisum was seated before the fireplace. When Starbuck entered the den, it was as though the old man hadn't moved since his last visit. Even the cheery glow of the fire did nothing to improve the rancher's jaundiced color. He still looked wasted and frail, a husk of his former self. Yet there was a noticeable change in his manner. He was smiling, and there was a peculiar glint in his eyes.

"By golly!" Chisum boomed, pumping his arm with vigor. "Good to see you, Luke! We were mighty impressed with the way you jumped right in there and helped nail the Kid. Ain't that right, Sallie?"

"Yes, Father." Sallie paused beside his chair, smiling. "And very grateful, too."

Her hair was parted in the middle, pulled back in a tight bun. The effect was severe, but somehow accented her fine features when she smiled. She gently touched her father, placing a hand on his shoulder as if he were a fragile artifact beyond value. The gesture was natural yet revealing. Watching her, Starbuck had the impression she would never marry while her father lived. After he'd taken a seat, she excused herself and left the room. The instant the door closed, Chisum hunched forward, chortling softly.

"Tell me all about it! Skinned the little bastard good and proper, did you?"

Starbuck gave him a clenched smile. "The Kid sent you a message."

"Oh?" Chisum inquired. "What's that?"

"He said to take your deal and stuff it. He doesn't believe you'd keep your word, and he trusts the governor only about as far as he could throw him."

Chisum eyed him with a mixture of dismay and surprise. "How'd you find out?"

"Secrets of the trade." Starbuck lolled back, hooked one leg over the chair arm. "I suppose you had your reasons, but I didn't come all this way to see the Kid get a life sentence. I want him hung, and one way or another, I aim to get the job done. So I'll trade you some information in return for your promise not to interfere any further."

"What sort of information?"

"Dobson and a fellow named Joe Coghlin are behind the rustling. They use Coghlin's slaughterhouse to get rid of the rustled stock."

"The Kid told you that?"

Starbuck related the gist of his conversation with the Kid. Chisum merely listened, coldly silent. His frown deepened when he heard the Kid had refused to give evidence against Dobson and Coghlin. But he agreed, after some argument, to leave the young outlaw to the courts. He frankly admitted he'd never had much influence with the governor anyway. Then, almost as an afterthought, Starbuck casually changed the subject.

"You know anything about the Santa Fe Land and Development Company?"

"What makes you ask?"

"Curiosity." Starbuck watched for a reaction. "Got an idea there's a connection between Judge Hough and the president of that outfit, Warren Mitchell."

Chisum's face was arrested in shock. "Hough? Owen Hough? Are you sure?"

Starbuck briefly described the incident in Santa Fe. He told of spotting Hough, and then the man with the waxed mustache, slipping out of the feed store. He went on to relate how he'd followed the man to the offices over the bank. The facts, he concluded, spoke for themselves. Judge Hough and Warren Mitchell—whatever their reasons—were meeting in secret.

Chisum's features were now drawn and solemn.

"Have you ever heard of the Santa Fe Ring?"

"No." Starbuck shook his head. "Not that I recollect."

"They're a group of businessmen and bankers. A small group, but the real power behind the scenes. Their purpose is to gain political and economic control of the territory. All of it—including the Pecos Valley!"

"And I take it you've stopped them?"

"So far." Chisum was visibly shaken. "I always thought they were behind the Lincoln County War. But I couldn't prove it, and then the truce come along and I hoped we'd seen the last of it. Looks like I was wrong."

"You're saying Hough and the rustling are all tied in some way to this Santa Fe Ring?"

Chisum nodded. "Never occurred to me that Hough was their man, but it makes sense. Don't you see, they're afraid to kill me outright. Too much blood's been spilled around here already. So they'll wait for me to die, and Hough will have it all set up to take over control of the valley. Goddamn vultures!"

"Pretty cagey," Starbuck remarked. "Once you're gone, they'll own New Mexico kit and caboodle."

"Appears that way." The cattleman paused, looking Starbuck over like a prize bull he was considering buying. "Course, if you were willin' to lend a hand . . ."

"Not my fight," Starbuck said evenly. "I got the Kid, and that finishes it so far as I'm concerned."

"Does it?" Chisum studied his nails, thoughtful a moment. "You know, the Kid only pulled the trigger. The others—Dobson and Coghlin—their hands are just as dirty. If they hadn't made rustlin' worthwhile, then Ben Langham and the Kid probably wouldn't've never crossed trails."

"That's dirty pool."

"Maybe." Chisum's tone was severe. "But it's the God's truth, and you know it just as sure as you're sittin' there."

Starbuck stared at him, considering. "What was it you had in mind?"

"Look into things, investigate it. Maybe you'd figure some way to put the screws to Dobson and Coghlin. If they ever broke, we'd be plumb certain to send the others runnin'."

"Well—" Starbuck shrugged, one eyebrow raised. "I guess it would take up the slack time while I'm waiting on the Kid to hang."

"That's the ticket!" Chisum grinned. "You open up that can of worms and there's no tellin' where it'll lead!"

"Hold off!" Starbuck corrected him. "I'll look into the rustling operation, but it stops there. Your political squabbles—the Santa Fe Ring and all that business—that's none of my affair. Let's make damn sure we understand one another on that score."

Chisum readily agreed. He smiled, bobbing his head, not in the least concerned. Age had taught him that certain men never did anything by halfway measures. Luke Starbuck would go all the way, and stick to the very last.

Early next morning Starbuck and Garrett dismounted outside the slaughterhouse. Starbuck's insistence on a search had put the lawman in a crabby mood. According to him, Coghlin slaughtered no more than fifty head a month, supplying the butcher-shop trade in Lincoln and nearby towns. That accounted for less than half the cows rustled from the Jinglebob, not to mention an equal number stolen each month in the Panhandle. He thought the search was a waste of time, and altogether the wrong way to start an investigation. Starbuck, listening with only one ear, had remained adamant.

Entering the office, they found Coghlin poring over an accounting ledger. A squat, fat man with sagging jowls, he had deep-set eyes and a down-turned mouth. He looked up, stubbing out a cigarette with nicotine-stained fingers, and rose from the desk. His expression was neutral.

After a round of handshakes, Coghlin congratulated them on their capture of the Kid. He evidenced no surprise when introduced to Starbuck, commenting blandly that everyone in Lincoln had heard of the new deputy. On edge, Garrett cut short the small talk with a curt gesture.

"Mind if we have a look around, Joe?"

"Look around?" Coghlin suddenly frowned. "What for?"

"I'll tell you if we find it."

"C'mon now, Sheriff! That's a little high-handed, don't you think?"

"Not unless you got something to hide."

"No, I don't," Coghlin blustered. "On the other hand, you've got no right busting in here without some kind of authorization."

"Well, it's like this, Joe." Garrett paused, fixed him with a scowl. "You force me to get a search warrant and I'm gonna be awful put out. Why not cooperate and save yourself some grief?"

Coghlin stared at them for several seconds. Then he shrugged, still frowning. "All right," he said crossly. "Where would you like to start?"

"Your hide pile," Starbuck broke in, silencing Garrett with a look. "We'll skip the rest."

Coghlin mumbled an inaudible reply. He led them outside, and walked toward the rear of the building. Behind the slaughterhouse, stacks of dried cowhides awaited shipment to the tannery. In all, flattened stiff and boardlike, there were perhaps a hundred hides. Halting, Coghlin motioned with a disdainful wave.

"Help yourself."

Starbuck moved forward, and began a systematic inspection of the hides. One at a time, removing them from the stacks, he checked each hide front and back. His expression became increasingly somber as he worked his way from stack to stack. Then, near the bottom of the last stack, he grunted softly.

Holding a cowhide in front of him, he walked to where Garrett and Coghlin waited.

"There's your proof."

Tapping the hide, he directed Garrett's attention to the brand. On the hair side the marking was a distinct □X. He flipped the hide over, revealing a clearly legible LX on the underside. He dropped the hide on the ground.

"The brand's been altered," he said. "Somebody used a running iron to change the L into a box. Only one trouble, though. The original brand burns all the way through, and there's no way to change it on the back side." He kicked the hide with the toe of his boot. "That cow came off of Langham's spread, over in the Panhandle."

"Spot anything off the Jinglebob?"

"No," Starbuck admitted. "Only the one had been altered."

"One hide," Garrett said thoughtfully. "That ain't much in the way of evidence, Luke."

"Maybe." Starbuck turned his gaze on Coghlin. "I understand you've got a ranch a few miles outside town."

"So?"

"You have any objection to our taking a look-see?"

"A look-see?" Coghlin repeated, stealing a glance at Garrett. "What's all this about, Sheriff?"

"Seems pretty clear," Garrett observed. "Somebody's been rustlin' stock."

"You're accusing me of rustling?"

"Nope, never said that."

"Well, it's a damn good thing! I'm in the business of buying cows, but I'm no expert on altered brands. Outside of stock detectives and cow thieves, not many people are."

"Which clears you on both counts, don't it?"

"You bet your life it does!"

"Then you won't have no objection to my deputy ridin' out there, will you, Joe?"

"I guess not," Coghlin said grudgingly. "When did you have in mind?"

"Today," Starbuck told him. "Sooner the better, and it'd probably be a good idea if you tagged along."

Coghlin averted his eyes. "Sorry, but I have business here in town. I'll give you a note to my foreman, Earl Gantry. He runs the spread for me anyway."

"Whatever seems fair."

Starbuck gave the cowhide another kick, then walked off. He knew, almost instinctively, that Coghlin's foreman would receive two notes. One he carried, and one sent ahead in warning. He planned to ride within the hour.

By late afternoon Starbuck's case looked stronger. With John Poe and their four men, he had spent several hours combing the rangeland on Coghlin's spread. The tally was encouraging, if not altogether conclusive. From scattered bunches of cows, they had cut out eight head with altered brands. Three were originally Jinglebob stock, and five had once worn the brands of various ranches in the Panhandle.

Earl Gantry, Coghlin's ramrod, had dogged their tracks throughout the afternoon. As Starbuck suspected, he had been warned in advance, and he went out of his way to make their job more difficult. Any question was met with an evasive reply, and he flatly refused to discuss all matters pertaining to operation of the ranch. Like a shadow, he simply stuck with them, watching their every move.

Shortly before sundown, Starbuck halted the search and rode back to the ranch compound. He realized now that it would take time to comb Coghlin's entire spread. There was the further problem of holding the rustled stock until identification could be made and officially registered with the Stockgrowers' Association. Yet all that was secondary to the larger problem. The case against Coghlin was strong, but wholly circumstantial.

Several factors worked to Coghlin's advantage. The cowhide at the slaughterhouse was, in itself, not particularly damning. The rustled stock at the ranch proved possession but not intent. Coghlin would doubtless contend he had bought the cows in good faith, unaware of the altered brands. And to cap it, Starbuck himself had soured the Kid on turning state's evidence. There was no corroboration, and therefore nothing substantial to establish Joe Coghlin's guilt.

And there the link to Jack Dobson ended. Judge Owen Hough, whatever his complicity, seemed almost untouchable.

At the compound, Starbuck noticed an older woman and a buxom young girl standing outside the house. But his attention was quickly diverted. As he stepped down out of the saddle, Gantry kneed his horse closer.

"You got more business here, Deputy?"

"Lots more," Starbuck said quietly. "I aim to spend the night, and I'd appreciate some grub for my men."

"The hell you say!"

Gantry had cold gunmetal eyes, sleek muddy hair and weatherbeaten features. He was muscular, somewhat taller than Starbuck, and had the lean hips of a horseman. The challenge in his voice was unmistakable.

"Mr. Gantry," Starbuck said, eyes boring into him, "I'd advise you not to mess with the law. I intend to comb your herds and collect any cows with altered brands. That's called evidence, and you'll put yourself in the position of obstructing justice if you try to stop me."

"Well—" Gantry blinked, suddenly uncertain of his ground. "Have you cleared that with Mr. Coghlin?"

"I don't need to clear it with him. The cows are stolen and I'm within my rights as an officer of the law."

"By God, we'll just see about that!"

Gantry reined his horse sharply around. He spurred hard and rode off at a gallop toward town. Watching him disappear down the road, Starbuck was tempted to lag back and follow him into Lincoln. A war council would almost certainly be called tonight, and a roster of those who attended might prove useful at some later date. Aside from Judge Hough, Starbuck was curious if there were other townspeople who still supported the Dobson faction. Then, out of the corner of his eye, he saw a man approach the house. The woman and the girl greeted him, and together they trooped inside. Any thought of trailing Gantry suddenly vanished. Instead, his thoughts turned to the older couple and the girl, obviously a family.

He wondered if they'd ever met Billy the Kid.

CHAPTER 9

Ellen Nesbeth was twenty years old. A girl in the eyes of her parents, she was actually a woman of experience, with no small insight into the ways of men. She knew, while watching Gantry and the deputy exchange words, that the deliverance she yearned for was about to happen. Her one hope was that it might be done without complications.

Fred and Erma Nesbeth, her parents, hadn't the faintest notion that Earl Gantry was her lover. She was a blonde tawny cat of a girl, with a sumptuous figure and a sultry manner. Her eyes were bold, large and expressive, yet bright with intelligence, and provocative. She lacked orthodox beauty, but her short impudent nose and her wide smiling mouth did nothing to lessen her impact on men. She was a stunning woman, and though her parents believed her to be naïve, she thought of herself as an enchantress. She liked the way men looked at her, and she had never once regretted her loss of innocence.

She deeply regretted, however, that her innocence had been wasted on Earl Gantry. In the beginning, she wanted only to escape the tedium and meager existence of her parents' world. She thought Gantry was her ticket to a life of excitement and forbidden comfort. A year ago, with a calculation that belied her age, she had allowed him to seduce her. Afterwards, when it was too late, she discovered he was a brutal man, vindictive and sometimes cruel. Because he was a braggart, forever attempting to impress her, she also discovered he was a thief. By then, her illusion of a new life shattered, she understood she had made a mistake. She could control him with feminine wile, and her body, but there seemed little hope she would ever escape him. Until today.

And now, helping her mother clear the supper dishes, her thoughts centered on that possibility. She was not a mean or spiteful person. While she connived, often manipulating those around her, there was no intent to hurt anyone. But tonight all that had changed. Her most fervent wish was that Earl Gantry would be arrested and sent to prison. The idea loomed before her like salvation itself. She saw it as her only chance, perhaps her last chance.

Yet, for all her wishful thinking, she was a realist. However much she wanted Gantry out of her life, she would do nothing to speed his downfall. She believed him capable of any act, not excluding cold-blooded murder. And anyone who betrayed him would do so at their own peril. She hoped the chief deputy—the one with the hard features and the measured voice—would expose Gantry, and take him off to jail. But she had thought it out quite clearly, and if asked, she would utter no word of condemnation against Earl Gantry. Death was not the escape she had envisioned for herself.

A knock broke the thread of her reverie. Her father, who was seated beside a pot-bellied stove, rose and crossed the kitchen. Even before he opened the door, some dark complex of intuition and dread told her it was the chief deputy. Then the door swung open, and he stood revealed in a spill of light.

"Evening."

"Evenin', Deputy." Fred Nesbeth stepped aside. "Come in out of the cold."

"Thanks."

Starbuck entered the kitchen, removing his hat. Nesbeth introduced his wife and daughter, and Starbuck nodded politely. His eyes touched on Ellen, and she sensed he was a good deal more clever than he appeared. With Gantry in town, he obviously meant to make the most of opportunity. Then her father offered him a chair, and the two men took seats before the stove.

"Well, now, Deputy," Nesbeth said affably. "What can we do for you?"

"If you don't mind, I'd like to ask you a few questions."

Ellen felt a sudden stab of alarm. Her father was a slender man, with the look of a rumpled sparrow, and altogether too trusting for his own good. He had eager brown eyes, a warm smile, and an almost compulsive need to please. To her knowledge, he had never told a lie in his life, and his simple-hearted honesty often worked to his own misfortune. She waited with mounting apprehension.

"Ask away," Nesbeth said agreeably. "I don't know as I'll be able to help you, but I'll sure give'er a try."

"Oh, it's just routine."

Starbuck took a stub pencil and a tally book from his coat pocket. He flipped to a clean page in the tally book and wet the tip of the pencil on his tongue. Watching him, Ellen was almost taken in by his artless performance. She moved closer to her father.

"Now, let's see, Mr. Nesbeth. The boys down at the bunkhouse tell me you're sort of the jack-of-all-trades around here. Would that pretty much describe your job?"

"Sure would!" Nesbeth chortled. "Fix anything, that's my line of work. Wagons, windmills, implements, you name it and I'll figger out what makes it tick. Pretty fair blacksmith, too. Always had the gift for workin' with my hands."

"And Mrs. Nesbeth?" Starbuck made another entry in the tally book. "I understand she looks after the main house, and does the cooking for Gantry and Mr. Coghlin."

"Yep, that's right, housekeeper and cook. Makes the choicest sourdough biscuits you ever popped in your mouth, don't you, Erma?"

Erma Nesbeth was a small woman, tending to middle-age spread, her skin prematurely lined by the plains sun. The crow's feet around her eyes gave her a perpetually worried expression, and she seldom smiled. She glanced up from the basin, nodding to her husband's question. Then she went on washing dishes.

"Anyone else live here?" Starbuck inquired easily. "Besides you folks and your daughter?"

"Well, Gantry's not married, and Mr. Coghlin's a widower, so that about does it."

"How about guests? Mr. Coghlin entertain a lot, does he?"

"No, not much. Few folks from town, now and then."

"Jack Dobson? Judge Hough? His business associates?"

"Oh, sure, they've stayed to supper a time or two."

Starbuck studied his tally book. "How about Billy Bonney?"

"The Kid?" Nesbeth laughed, shook his head. "No, the Kid never stayed to supper."

"But he's been here, hasn't he? Some of the hands told me they've seen him around the place lots of times."

"Why, sure, he's—"

"*No!*" Ellen Nesbeth hurried to her father. "Daddy, he's trying to trap you! No one told him anything. They wouldn't dare!"

Starbuck had to admire the girl's spunk. She spoke with a firmness that surprised him, and she had also read his hand perfectly. He was bluffing like a penny-ante cardsharp. The boys in the bunkhouse hadn't given him the time of day.

"Miss Nesbeth," he addressed her with a stern look, "it doesn't matter what anybody else told me. You've just confirmed that the Kid has been a guest in this house. The guest of Joe Coghlin."

"I did not!" She bridled. "You're putting words in my mouth!"

"I don't understand," Nesbeth said vaguely. "What's all the to-do about the Kid? He never made no trouble here."

"Oh, Daddy!" Ellen cried. "Hush up! Just hush up! You're only making it worse."

"No, ma'am, you're wrong," Starbuck said in a deliberate voice. "It couldn't get any worse."

She stared at him with shocked round eyes. "What do you mean?"

"I mean you and your folks are in bad trouble. You're accessories before the fact to the crimes of rustling and murder. That makes you as guilty as Coghlin and Gantry, and the Kid, too."

He saw anger, confusion, and a trace of fear in her eyes. She glared at him. "You're lying! You can't prove a thing!"

"Oh, I've got the proof," Starbuck lied, deadpan. "Why do you think Gantry hightailed it into town? No, it's not a matter of proof, Miss Nesbeth. From now on, we're just choosing up sides to see who stays out of jail."

"Jail?" Nesbeth asked in a hoarse whisper. "Mister, what in tarnation are you talkin' about?"

Starbuck leaned forward, his tone earnest. "I'm saying your boss is a thief, Mr. Nesbeth. He hired the Kid to do his rustling, and the Kid killed some people in the process, and that makes everybody who works here answerable to the law. Now, maybe you weren't in on it—"

"Of course he wasn't!" Ellen said fiercely. "He never knew a thing! You just have to look at him to tell that."

"Maybe so." Starbuck's face suddenly turned hard, as though cast in metal. "But the law don't make exceptions. Unless you folks come forward and agree to testify, then you're open to the same charges as Coghlin and everybody else."

"Testify!" Ellen flared. "Don't listen to him, Daddy! He's trying to scare you. We're not guilty of anything!"

Words appeared to fail Nesbeth. He looked from his daughter to Starbuck, completely undone by the thought of jail. There was a prolonged silence, broken only by the hiss of flames in the stove. Then, turning from the wash basin, Erma Nesbeth spoke for the first time.

"Fred, you do what the man says. We been living in a nest of vipers and we all knew it. No sense fooling yourself any longer."

"Oh God, Mama!" Ellen stared at her, aghast. "Are you crazy? Do you know what you're doing?"

"I know lots of things." Mrs. Nesbeth looked her up and down. "Things that shamed me, and sometimes made me wish you wasn't my own flesh and blood." She paused, tears welling up in her eyes. "It's time we got out of here. Way past time."

Ellen turned away, her face livid. For a moment no one spoke, and then, glancing at his wife, Nesbeth seemed to pull himself together. He cleared his throat, swallowed hard.

"Just exactly what is it you're askin', Mr. Starbuck?"

"I want you to make a deposition. Tell everything you know, get it down in writing, and sign it."

"And my womenfolk, nothin' will happen to them?"

"Not to them or you, Mr. Nesbeth. You have my word on it."

"Awright, Deputy, you got yourself a witness."

John Poe brought a buckboard and team to the house an hour after sunup. Starbuck stood outside the kitchen door, waiting on the Nesbeths to appear. To avoid trouble, he had delayed their departure until the bunkhouse emptied and the hands went off about their daily chores. He walked forward as Poe climbed down from the buckboard.

Late last night, he had explained the situation to Poe and the men. He believed it essential that the Nesbeths be removed from the ranch as quickly as possible. One reason was precautionary, a matter of their personal safety. Another was the girl, who from all indications had fallen under Gantry's influence. Once he had them safely in Lincoln, and had taken a deposition, he would return to the ranch. Poe and the men, meanwhile, were to continue combing Coghlin's herds. He wanted the rustled stock gathered and ready for inspection no later than tomorrow afternoon.

Starbuck halted where he could keep an eye on the house. He nodded to Poe. "Any trouble?"

"Nope." Poe shifted his quid and spat. "Most everybody had cleared out when I went to hitch up the team. Course, I had a little starin' contest with Gantry at breakfast."

"He was in the cook shack?"

"Bigger'n life," Poe noted. "For what it's worth, he looked like he'd just swallowed a couple of dozen canaries. You reckon he got some fresh orders in Lincoln last night?"

"We'll see," Starbuck said, glancing toward the cook shack. "Here he comes now."

Earl Gantry hurried across the compound. He moved with a determined stride, his expression one of sharp annoyance. Halting in front of Starbuck, he indicated the buckboard.

"What's the idea?"

"Borrowing your buckboard," Starbuck remarked. "I'll drop it off with Coghlin when I'm done."

"Why do you need a buckboard?"

Starbuck ignored the question. "I'm leaving Deputy Poe in charge. Him and the boys know what to do, and I'd suggest you stay out of their way."

"That still don't tell me why—"

Gantry stopped, his eyes suddenly hooded. He stared toward the house, watching with disbelief as the Nesbeths appeared at the kitchen door. Ellen carried a small valise, and her father struggled along with two heavy carpetbags. Mrs. Nesbeth, clutching an ancient mantle cloak to her bosom, brought up the rear.

"Gantry," Starbuck said quietly, "I'm taking the Nesbeths into custody. I'd advise you not to make any trouble."

"You're not takin' nobody unless you've got a warrant."

"I won't say it again—"

"Back inside!" Gantry shouted. He jerked his thumb at the house, and took a step toward the Nesbeths. "You heard me! Get the hell—"

Starbuck lashed out in a fast shadowy movement. He exploded two splintering punches on the jaw, a left hook followed by a clubbing right cross. Gantry went down as though his legs had been chopped from beneath him. He struck the ground and lay still, out cold.

Hardly winded, Starbuck motioned the Nesbeths to the buckboard and got them seated. He walked to the hitchrack, where his horse was tied, and mounted. Gathering the reins, he shifted in the saddle and looked back at Poe.

"John," he said in a low voice, "if our friend wants to argue about it when he wakes up, you give him some more of the same."

"I'll do'er, Luke," Poe grinned. "You watch out for yourself, you hear me?"

"I always do."

Starbuck nodded to Fred Nesbeth, and reined his horse around. With the buckboard trundling along behind, he rode toward Lincoln.

A chill winter haze obscured the sun. Starbuck consulted his pocketwatch, estimating time and distance. By rough reckoning, he figured they were halfway to Lincoln. Ahead, the road snaked past a boulder-strewn butte, descending gradually to a level plain. At the latest, he judged they would reach town by the noon hour.

Since departing the ranch, Starbuck hadn't exchanged a dozen words with the Nesbeths. Crowded into the lone buckboard seat, they looked solemn as molting owls. The girl was especially somber. She kept her eyes turned away from him, and he sensed she had been shaken by the way he'd manhandled Gantry. He felt some vague need to explain himself, the necessity to strike first and strike hard when confronted by a troublemaker. But he suppressed the urge. The Nesbeths and their daughter would never understand that violence was a part of his trade. When words failed, he used his fists. Or in the last resort, he used a gun. Certain men, unpersuaded by reason, left him no alternative. Only a fool allowed the other man the first blow.

Starbuck had ridden most of the morning beside

the buckboard. But now, as the road narrowed through a rocky defile, he waved Nesbeth on and drifted to the rear. His thoughts turned to details. He wondered if the county would pay to quarter the Nesbeths at the hotel. If not, then he would have to work out some arrangement with Chisum. There was also the question of round-the-clock guards. He didn't fool himself on that score, though he'd said nothing to the Nesbeths. Their lives were in jeopardy, and in the days to come, there would be no substitute for vigilance. He grunted softly to himself, struck by an unpleasant thought. He wondered if Garrett could be entrusted with the guard detail. It was no job for a tyro, and the sheriff was very definitely—

His saddlehorn suddenly blew apart.

A split second later he heard the gunshot, and then another. A slug fried the air past his left ear, and he saw a puff of smoke in the boulders directly ahead. All in an instant he realized he was trapped between two bushwhackers. One was to the front, and the other was on his immediate right, hidden in the rocks. He spurred his horse into a gallop, aware that Nesbeth was whipping the team. Slugs were pocking the earth all around him, and the blast of rifle fire quickened to an earsplitting drumroll. He knew then he had no chance of outrunning the ambush. His only choice was to stand and fight.

Yanking his carbine from its scabbard, he hauled back on the reins with savage force. His horse skidded to a halt, almost squatting on its haunches, and he jumped from the saddle. The sudden stop caught the bushwhackers by surprise; their fire slackened, and he blocked off the one on his right flank by crouching beside his horse. He jacked a shell into the carbine, and centered the sights on the spot where he'd seen a puff of smoke. A rifle muzzle was laid over the boulder, then the crown of a hat appeared and a man rose slightly to shift his aim. For an instant, bobbing up for a better look, his head was visible. Starbuck shot him between the eyes.

Whirling around, Starbuck stepped past his horse, and in the same motion, dropped to one knee. A slug whistled over his head, and on the rocky knoll to the right, he saw the second bushwhacker. Working the lever, he triggered a half dozen rounds into the rocks. The spang of ricochets spread across the knoll like a swarm of bees. Then, before he could steady his sights, a man leaped from behind a rock and dove headfirst over the knoll. He touched off another shot for good measure and rose to his feet, waiting. A moment later he heard the faint sound of hoofbeats, then nothing.

Starbuck caught a stirrup and scrambled into the saddle. Some distance ahead, he saw the buckboard jouncing down the road. He roweled his horse in the ribs and took off at a dead lope. Once clear of the defile, he jammed his carbine into the saddle scabbard.

In the heat of the fight, he'd had no time to think things through. But as he pounded after the buckboard all the pieces began falling into place. He realized the ambush had been arranged as a warning to the Nesbeths. Though they were sitting ducks in the buckboard, all the gunfire had been directed at him. Which meant Gantry had ordered the ambush only after he'd departed the ranch with the Nesbeths in custody. It made perfect sense. By cutting cross-country, the bushwhackers had easily gotten ahead of the slow-moving buckboard. Had Gantry selected cooler men—and better shots—he would now be dead.

Yet, for all that, there was an element of still greater consequence. Gantry would never have ordered the ambush on his own. Coghlin and Dobson, perhaps even Judge Hough, had met with the ranch foreman last night. One or all of them had clearly authorized him to take whatever steps he considered necessary. Killing a law officer was serious business, and the repercussions would have been felt all the way to Santa Fe. They were desperate men, willing to resort to desperate measures, and the conclusion was inescapable. Having failed to kill him, they wouldn't hesitate to kill the Nesbeths. The next try would be better planned and more skillfully executed. Unless he found sanctuary of some sort, there was no doubt as to the outcome. All the Nesbeths, the girl included, would be murdered.

When Starbuck overtook the buckboard, he signaled a change in direction. He turned east, across the plains, on a course that would bypass Lincoln entirely. He led the Nesbeths toward the Pecos, and the Jinglebob. To the man who more than any other needed them alive.

CHAPTER 10

"Politics be damned!"

"Easy to say," Chisum commented. "But politics are a hard fact of life. You can kick up all the dust you want, and it won't change a thing."

"That's about the lamest excuse I ever heard."

"Luke, I don't make the rules. If I had my choice, we'd go back to the way it was in the old days. Things was a damnsight easier when we didn't have so much law, and nobody knows it better than me."

"Over in the Panhandle we've got our own law. Anyone steps out of line and he gets what's coming to him—pronto."

"I don't doubt it for a minute. Dog-eat-dog and devil take the hindmost, ain't that about it?"

"Why not?" Starbuck said harshly. "Skip all the legal hocus-pocus, and keep it simple. That's the only kind of law most folks understand anyway."

Chisum marked again that the younger man was something of a cynic. "Well, Luke, I guess that's the price we pay for civilization. The law gets more and more complicated, and common folks wind up not havin' a helluva lot to say about the way things are run. Course, when you core the apple, it's all politics. A few people call the tune, and the rest of us spend our lives tryin' to keep time with the music."

"Politics or not, I still say we've got a case."

"And I repeat," Chisum emphasized, "where politics are involved, it has to be airtight and wrapped in a red ribbon."

"Jesus!" Starbuck muttered. "We've got the stolen cows and we've got the Nesbeths. What more do you want?"

"It's all circumstantial, Luke! Even the Nesbeths admit they never really heard anything. They saw Coghlin and the Kid together, and they saw money exchange hands a couple of times. So what's that prove?"

"How many times do I have to tell you? It ties Coghlin to the Kid and the rustled cows."

"Sure it does," Chisum nodded, "so far as you and me are concerned. But any grand jury impaneled in Lincoln won't be impartial about it. Lots of people are politically aligned with Dobson and Coghlin, and they're not gonna return an indictment unless we show 'em some rock-hard evidence." He paused, reflective a moment. "Besides, we ain't got nothin' on Owen Hough, and he's the one joker I don't aim to let slip past. Without him, we're just dealin' in small fry, and there ain't no way that'll put an end to it."

"The rustling," Starbuck asked, one eyebrow lifted, "or the politics?"

"Both," Chisum said firmly. "There ain't no way to separate one from the other. That's what I've been tryin' to get through your head since we started talkin'."

Starbuck scrubbed his face with his palms. Last night, when he'd delivered the Nesbeths to the Jinglebob, there seemed to him no loose ends. He had their testimony, and along with the rustled stock, that made the case against Coghlin. Today, all the loose ends had come unraveled.

The problem was John Chisum. The cattleman had readily agreed that the Nesbeths were a valuable, and unexpected, asset. He had them quartered in the main house, and assigned men to guard them night and day. No less than the Nesbeths, uncovering the stolen cows also drew his praise. A messenger was dispatched ordering Poe to drive the cows into Lincoln; there an inspector from the Stockgrowers' Association would verify that the brands had been altered. All last evening, in fact, Chisum had been in fine spirits. He marveled that so much had been accomplished in three days, and commended Starbuck on a remarkable piece of detective work. But this morning, completely reversing himself, he had argued against pressing charges. Politics, like war, demanded total victory. He wanted Owen Hough—or nothing.

Oddly enough, Starbuck had undergone a change himself. After retiring last night, he'd been unable to sleep for a long while. Something about the ambush bothered him, and his thoughts slowly turned to Coghlin and Dobson. Over the past four years, any number of men had tried to kill him; the attempts were viewed impersonally, for he understood it was the nature of outlaws to fight when cornered. An assassination, however, was an altogether different matter. For the first time, someone had ordered his murder, authorized his death by *name*. That seemed to him very personal, and not to be tolerated.

The Kid still had priority. Events of the last few days had in no way affected the determination to see him hung. Yet the more Starbuck pondered it, the more he realized the Kid was merely the tool of ambitious men. And those men were by far the greater evil. Their use of corruption and murder to achieve power was on a scale incomprehensible to anyone not personally touched by it. Lying awake, struck by this new perspective of things, Starbuck gradually became intrigued with the Santa Fe Ring. As a detective, the thought of bringing them to justice was irresistible, a professional challenge. On the personal side of the ledger, he needed no excuse. These men had ordered him killed. *By name!* Which was reason enough to follow the trail wherever it might lead. To Coghlin and Dobson, and then, without question, to Judge Hough. And perhaps beyond, to the men in Santa Fe.

Thinking on it now, he wondered why he was resisting Chisum. The logical next step was to go after Dobson, and before sleep had claimed him last night, he'd come to the same conclusion himself.

Perhaps it was nothing more than stubborn pride. He had an aversion to taking orders, and Chisum wasn't the most tactful man he'd run across. Whatever the cause, he suddenly realized he was being not only bullheaded, but short-sighted as well. He stared at the rancher a moment longer, then shrugged.

"Go ahead," he said without expression, "I'm all ears. What's your idea?"

Chisum sensed a change in attitude. He hitched forward in his chair, watching the younger man closely. "The Kid's the key to everything. With his testimony, we'd have Coghlin by the short hairs, and more'n likely that would open the door to Dobson. Do you agree?"

"Let's say I do," Starbuck allowed. "How do we get the Kid to talk?"

"Well, for the moment, we just sit tight. We keep the Nesbeths under wraps, and we don't say nothin' more about the rustled stock. Coghlin won't know what the hell we've got in mind, and that'll make him sweat all the more. So we let him sweat, and meantime, we wait for the Kid to be sentenced to hang. At that point—"

"Hold on," Starbuck interrupted. "You told me there's no chance of commutation."

"No chance at all," Chisum affirmed. "Course, we'll let him think we're still tryin', and at the same time we'll convince him his friends ain't turned a hand to save him. Which won't be no lie. I've got a hunch Coghlin and Dobson want to see him swing more'n we do."

"So we tell him he's been betrayed, turn him against Coghlin."

"And once he talks, we use that to turn Coghlin against Dobson."

"Then we offer Dobson a deal to spill the beans on Judge Hough."

"And one by one, we work our way up the line. Even if all of 'em don't crack, somebody's bound to lead us to the boys in Santa Fe. That's the payoff, and I say the odds favor us blowin' the whole mess wide apart."

A smile tugged at the corner of Starbuck's mouth. "Anybody ever tell you you're a devious old bastard?"

Chisum laughed. "I don't reckon you'd be the first."

"Probably won't be the last, either."

"By God, I hope not, Luke. I shorely do!"

There was a knock at the door. Sallie Chisum entered the den, and moved toward them. Her lips were set in a thin line, and she seemed attenuated, somehow on edge. She halted, looking from her father to Starbuck.

"We seem to have a problem with Miss Nesbeth."

"Oh?" Starbuck asked. "What's the trouble?"

Sallie flushed. "I'm afraid her language doesn't bear repeating. But to give you a loose translation, she refuses to stay cooped up in the house and she insists on being allowed to go for a ride."

"On horseback?"

"Yes," Sallie replied, her tone waspish. "And she had the nerve to ask if she could borrow a riding outfit. Honestly, some people! We're nowhere near the same size."

Starbuck had a strong suspicion they were nowhere near on anything. Sallie Chisum was a lady, with the genteel manner and refined air of someone accustomed to wealth. He had known only a few such women in his lifetime, and none of them intimately. But he had known hundreds of women like Ellen Nesbeth. Young hellions, they yearned for excitement and adventure, and one way or another, they always found it. Some made their way to the cowtowns, where they worked as dance hall girls, or chose a more lucrative profession in the parlor houses. The others, unable to escape home and family, devoted themselves to tantalizing the local farm boys or cowhands. These were the women who provoked fights at Saturday night dances, and thought themselves utter failures unless they had a string of admirers hanging on their every word. Their morals were questionable, and more often than not their bodies were used as instruments of emotional blackmail. Yet he understood them and, surprisingly, he enjoyed their company. Always a battle of wits, taming them was a spirited contest, never dull. To his way of thinking, it was not unlike skinning a faro dealer at a crooked table.

"I'll handle it," Starbuck said, rising from his

chair. "We have to keep Nesbeth happy, and like it or not, I suppose that means catering to his daughter."

He nodded to them, and walked from the room. Sallie's face reddened to the hairline. She avoided her father's eyes, seemingly struck speechless, her expression none too ladylike. Chisum suppressed a smile, and began fussing with his pipe.

Ellen Nesbeth wore a split riding skirt and a fleece-lined winter jacket. The outfit, borrowed from Sallie Chisum, was at least a size too small. Her breasts stood perfectly molded against the jacket, and the skirt stretched skin-tight across her buttocks. Walking down from the main house, she seemed oblivious to the stares of several Jinglebob hands loafing around the corral.

A grulla mare, one of Sallie Chisum's favorite mounts, had been saddled and brought from the stables. Starbuck waited beside his gelding, holding the reins to both horses. With a defiant look, Ellen ignored his greeting and snatched the mare's reins from his hand. When he offered to help her mount, she caught the stirrup with a practiced step and swung aboard the mare. For an instant, as her leg cleared the cantle, her fruity buttocks were outlined through the skirt. All eyes, the cowhands drew a breath in unison, their mouths ajar. She reined the mare around and rode off at a canter.

Starbuck mounted, laughing softly to himself,

and followed her south from the compound. He knew she had purposely put on a show for the men at the corral. She clearly delighted in flaunting her body, and an audience of leering cowhands added spice to the game. He thought it entirely likely that Sallie Chisum had lost her skirt for good.

When he rode up alongside her, Ellen slowed the mare to a walk. Surprised, he glanced at her, but she refused to meet his gaze. Her hair was drawn sleekly to the nape of her neck, tied with a ribbon, accentuating the smooth contours of her profile. She was a woman of surpassing beauty, with the bawdy eyes and sensuous mouth that certain men found compelling. Yet something in her carriage, the way her head tilted, brought to mind the old adage about vain women. He wondered if she got chapped lips from kissing cold mirrors.

A few miles from the house, Ellen reined to a halt on a slight rise. Before them, framed against the panorama of the Quadalupe Mountains, lay the Valley of Seven Rivers. She still hadn't spoken, and now, her eyes fixed upon distance, she studied the snowcapped spires beyond the valley. Starbuck hooked a leg around his saddlehorn, and rolled himself a smoke. He lit the cigarette, aware she could scarcely contain herself, but quite content to wait her out. Sooner or later they were bound to have words; and he knew the one thing she couldn't tolerate from any man was indifference. He provoked her with quiet disinterest.

"If I weren't a lady," she said at length, "you

would get your ears scorched six ways to Sunday."

"In that case," Starbuck exhaled a lazy stream of smoke, "let'er rip. I'm no gent and you're no lady, so why playact any different?"

"Bastard!" She invested the word with scorn. "You're the sorriest excuse for a man I've ever met."

"That and a nickel beer will get you a free lunch."

She was glaring at him now, face masked by anger. "You must be real proud of yourself. You lied to my folks—and scared them half out of their wits!—and then very nearly got them killed. Why couldn't you just leave well enough alone?"

"White lies don't count." Starbuck inspected the tip of his cigarette, flicked an ash. "Besides, those backshooters weren't after your folks anyway. Their orders were to get me."

"So what?" she said stiffly, her lips white. "Do you think I'm a fool? Next time they'll come after my folks—and me—and they won't miss. We're the targets now, not you."

"There won't be a next time. You're in protective custody, and you've got my word, no harm will come to you."

"Oh my God!" She laughed a tinny sound. "That's the biggest joke yet! What good is your word against bullets? Go on, Mr. Starbuck—tell me that!"

"Well, it's pretty simple from where I stand. Without your testimony, I'd never make a case. So

I don't aim to let anything happen to you."

"Really?" she said, lifting her chin. "And doesn't it bother you that a couple of people who never harmed anyone in their lives might end up dead? Do you sleep good at night, thinking about that?"

"I think about it," Starbuck said slowly, "but I don't lose any sleep. It's my job, and I do it the best way I know how."

"Your job!" She tossed her head. "Why, you're no better than the Kid! I weaseled it out of those dimwits guarding our rooms. You're a paid killer, Mr. Starbuck! A bounty hunter!"

Silence thickened between them. Starbuck assessed her with a cold, objective look. He was not a man who revealed his innermost feelings easily. His emotions were held under tight rein, and he was more apt to cover anything of a personal nature with an offhand remark. But her accusation stung, and there was a swiftly felt need to justify himself. He couldn't explain it, nor did he pause to think it through. He only knew it was important that Ellen Nesbeth not believe him to be a hired gun.

"I'm a manhunter," he said quietly, "but I don't take bounty. If the boys guarding your room told the whole story, then they must have told you I'm a range detective."

"I fail to see what difference that makes."

"In this case," Starbuck assured her, "it makes all the difference in the world. A few weeks ago the Kid murdered a man over in the Panhandle. His name was Ben Langham, and he was the best friend

I ever had. That's what brought me to New Mexico, that and nothing else."

"But the Kid's in jail! You caught him!"

"Yeah, but I've raised my sights since then. I want the man that hired the Kid, and the man that hired him. Coghlin and Dobson, and anybody else that had a hand in it. The whole bunch, top to bottom."

"You're crazy!" she said wildly. "You'll get yourself killed! You'll get us all killed!"

"No," Starbuck corrected her. "If there's any killing to be done, then I'm the one that'll do it."

Ellen Nesbeth stared at him, on the verge of saying something. Then she shook her head, her eyes suddenly sad and strangely bemused. She whirled the mare around with a sharp snap of the reins, and rode off. Starbuck kept her in sight all the way back to the ranch, but he made no attempt to overtake her. His mood was reflective, and he found himself troubled.

There was more to the girl than he'd expected, and her eyes told him things even she might not know. It was a disquieting thought.

CHAPTER 11

On the afternoon of April 12, William Bonney was led into the courtroom. An overflow crowd packed the benches, and several spectators shouted encouragement to the young outlaw. He waved, even though he was manacled hand and foot, and hobbled to the defense table. There, flanked by Garrett and Starbuck, he took a chair beside his attorney.

An air of tense expectation hung over the courtroom. The jury had retired late that morning, and now, after less than three hours' debate, they had reached a verdict. Opinion was divided among the onlookers; some thought a quick verdict would favor the Kid, while others believed it meant almost certain conviction. Either way, the sheriff of Dona Ana County was taking no chances with such a large crowd. Garrett and Starbuck had been assigned to guard the Kid, and local deputies were stationed at every door leading into the courtroom. Their orders were to move swiftly and decisively at the first sign of a demonstration.

The Kid, looking very cocksure, was perhaps the calmest person in the courtroom. Talking quietly

with his attorney, Arthur Fountain, he appeared un-
concerned about the verdict. Under the circumstances, many of those watching him thought it a
fine display of bravado. But it was no act, and his
bold manner was not meant to impress the spectators. He was, instead, utterly confident of acquittal.

To the Kid's way of thinking, the danger of a
guilty verdict had diminished step by step. Some
three months past he had been granted a change of
venue, with the trial scheduled to be held in the
town of Mesilla. Only a half day's ride from the
border, Mesilla was populated largely by Mexicans.
The people there had scarcely heard of the Lincoln
County War, and they cared even less about political vendettas. One gringo killing another was simply a matter of no consequence. Americans, in their
view, were all crazy.

All the more important, the process of jury se-
lection had resulted in twelve Mexicans sitting in
the jurors' box. The Kid could hardly credit his own
luck. Throughout the territory, Mexicans looked
upon him with respect and affection. He was known
to them as *El Chivato*, and wherever he rode, he'd
always been warmly welcomed into their homes.
Their attitude was influenced to no small degree by
his lukewarm manner toward Anglo women. He
much preferred dark-haired señoritas, and in that,
he was considered wise beyond his years. Quite
clearly, as he had demonstrated many times, he
trusted Mexicans more than he did his own people.
And they in turn counted it a mark of honor to have

shared a humble supper or a bottle of tequila with the young *bandido*.

The trial, begun only yesterday, had nonetheless given the Kid a few bad moments. Four eyewitnesses told essentially the same story. On a spring day in 1878 they had watched, horror-stricken, as the Kid and five members of his gang assassinated Sheriff William Brady. Crouched beside a building, the killers had caught the lawman on Lincoln's main street, and gunned him down without warning. Then, leaving nothing to chance, the Kid had coolly walked into the street and fired a final shot into the sheriff's head. The savagery of the act had been described in detail, and under cross-examination Arthur Fountain had done nothing to shake the witnesses' testimony. By late yesterday, when court had recessed, there seemed only one possible conclusion. William Bonney, with grisly premeditation, had murdered an officer of the law.

Earlier this morning, after closing arguments, the judge had charged the jury. When the twelve men filed out of the courtroom, there was little doubt, based on the evidence, as to their verdict. Yet now, waiting on them to return, the Kid appeared almost nonchalant. He simply couldn't believe an all-Mexican jury would convict him of anything.

"All rise!"

The bailiff's command brought everyone in the courtroom to his feet. Judge Walter Bristol emerged from the door to his chambers, and walked quickly to the bench. There was a moment of shuffling while the spectators resumed their seats, then the bailiff moved to a door behind the jury box. One by one, the jurors filed into the courtroom and took their chairs. None of them looked at the Kid.

Judge Bristol swiveled in their direction. "Gentlemen of the jury, have you reached a verdict?"

The jury foreman rose. "*Sí* . . . we have, Your Honor."

"Defendant will rise." The judge waited for the Kid and his attorney to stand, then glanced back at the foreman. "How do you find?"

"Guilty."

The foreman's mouth continued to move, but his words were lost in an outcry from the spectators. Garrett and Starbuck edged closer to the Kid, and the deputies posted around the room stood tensed, hands poised over their guns. Then the judge, banging his gavel, hammered the crowd into silence.

"Sentence will be pronounced at ten o'clock tomorrow morning. Court stands adjourned."

With a nod to the bailiff, Judge Bristol stepped down from the bench and disappeared into his chambers. The doors were thrown open, and at a signal from the sheriff, the deputies began clearing the courtroom. The crowd appeared unruly, darting sympathetic glances at the Kid and muttering among themselves. But the deputies, alert for trouble, herded them outside with a minimum of commotion.

The Kid looked as though he'd had the wind knocked out of him. His features were twisted in a grimace, and his eyes were vacant. He stared at the jury, watching with stunned bewilderment as they filed through the rear door. Once again, none of them met his gaze.

Arthur Fountain, who appeared somewhat sheepish, exchanged a few words with his client. Then, stuffing papers into his briefcase, the attorney hurried from the courtroom. Garrett and Starbuck fell in beside the Kid. The county jail was on the upper floor of the courthouse, and they walked him toward a door which led to the stairway.

"What's the matter, Billy?" Starbuck said as they moved through the door. "You look a little surprised."

"Go to hell."

"No need to get touchy. It wasn't me that let you down."

"What's that supposed to mean?"

"Why, it's simple enough," Starbuck observed. "Your friends got you a change of venue, and then let you sink or swim on your own. Isn't that about the size of it?"

"You're so smart, you tell me."

The Kid fell silent. The deal he'd struck while in the Santa Fe jail suddenly seemed shortsighted, and very unfair. He hadn't talked, and for that he had been spared a trial in Lincoln. But now, having been convicted, he knew there would be no further contact. He was on his own, with not the slightest hope of commutation. He felt alone and bitter, and he had a fleeting impression of the gallows. He sensed it was time to play his hole card.

On the second-story landing he turned to Starbuck. "Let's suppose I was ready to talk a deal. Your offer still open?"

"Depends on what you've got to trade."

"Joe Coghlin," the Kid said slowly. "And maybe enough to swing Dobson with him."

"Well—" Starbuck pursed his lips, thoughtful. "I reckon I could have a talk with Judge Bristol."

"Bristol?" The Kid's face congealed into a scowl. "What about the governor?"

"Waste of time," Starbuck remarked. "He couldn't do anything unless you'd already been sentenced. We're better off to take a crack at the judge." He paused, eyes narrowed in a squint. "Let's understand each other, Billy. I'll approach the judge; but whichever way it goes, I've got to have your word you'll still testify against Coghlin. Otherwise it's no deal."

"No monkey business," the Kid said sharply. "You make an honest try, and I'll hold up my end. But you try pullin' a fast one and all bets are off."

"Hell, Billy!" Starbuck mugged, hands outstretched. "You've got to learn to trust people. We're on the same side, now."

"Yeah, and bird dogs fly, too."

Garrett was silent throughout the exchange. Even after locking the Kid in his cell, the lawman seemed unusually thoughtful. But as they left the jail and approached the stairs, he looked at Starbuck.

126

"I understood Chisum had changed his mind about offerin' the Kid a deal."

"The way it worked out," Starbuck noted dryly, "he's the one that changed my mind."

"Oh?" Garrett asked. "How so?"

"He convinced me Coghlin and Dobson are more important than the Kid."

"How come I never heard nothin' about it?"

"Maybe you ought to ask Chisum."

Garrett flushed. "Well, for my money, he should've left well enough alone. I never agreed with the idea in the first place. What the territory needs is an object lesson, and believe you me, it'd do lots of folks a world of good to see the Kid strung up."

"I don't know about that"—Starbuck gave him a quick sidewise glance—"but it'd sure be a feather in your cap, wouldn't it, Pat?"

Garrett sputtered something under his breath and stalked off down the stairs. Watching him, Starbuck was amused by the lawman's artless and rather heavy-handed ambition. But privately, he had to admit he was in complete agreement. He too would have enjoyed seeing the Kid strung up.

Judge Walter Bristol was a man of stern visage and inflexible temperament. His head was leonine, with a shock of wavy white hair, and his eyes were unwavering behind thick spectacles. He gazed across the desk at Starbuck and Garrett.

"Let me understand you, Deputy." He laced his fingers together, peering over his glasses. "You're asking me to grant clemency as an inducement to make William Bonney testify against certain men alleged to be operating a rustling ring. Is that correct?"

"Yes, sir, it is," Starbuck acknowledged. "All the evidence we've turned up so far is circumstantial. Without Bonney's testimony, we'll probably never make a case."

"And that's all there is to it?" the judge demanded. "A gang of rustlers?"

"That's all, Your Honor," Starbuck lied, straight-faced. "Of course, I'd ask you to keep in mind, it's not just the rustling. These men are indirectly responsible for several of the murders committed by the Kid."

"I see." Judge Bristol eyed him, considering. "To be frank, Deputy, I'm not convinced. At bottom, everything in Lincoln County revolves around politics. I find it incredible that you would ask clemency for William Bonney—the worst desperado in the history of New Mexico Territory!—merely to convict a band of rustlers. I detect a nigger in the woodpile. One, quite probably, by the name of John Chisum."

"Chisum would benefit," Starbuck conceded, "but I don't think it's altogether politics. The Jinglebob makes a mighty inviting target for cow thieves."

"Indeed." The judge turned slowly to look at

Garrett. "Sheriff, you've had little to say on the matter, but I feel obligated to pose a question. Do you believe any form of clemency—even a life sentence in prison—would reform Billy the Kid?"

Garrett thought it over, and spoke carefully. "Judge, anything's possible. The Kid's young, and life on the rockpile might just straighten him out. But if you want my honest opinion, it ain't very likely."

Judge Bristol rose. "Thank you, Sheriff. I appreciate your candor. Now, if you gentlemen will excuse me, I have work to do." He gave Starbuck an owlish frown. "Deputy, you can tell John Chisum you made a game effort. That, at least, will be no lie."

Outside the judge's chambers, Garrett kept his eyes averted. As they walked through the courtroom, Starbuck thought it wholly in character that the lawman, forced to a choice, hadn't allowed loyalty to stand in the way of ambition. But he decided just as quickly that his story would be the same for both John Chisum and the Kid. He had made a game effort. And failed.

The following morning, precisely on the stroke of ten, Judge Bristol rapped his gavel and brought the court to order. The Kid, heavily manacled, stood before the bench. Adjusting his glasses, Judge Bristol studied the execution warrant a moment, and then set it aside. He looked down at the young out-law.

"Before I pass sentence, have you anything you wish to say?"

"Damn right!" the Kid declared sullenly. "A whole bunch of fellows did just as much killin' as me up in Lincoln County. But they're walkin' around free as you please and no worries. How come I'm the only one that gets sent to the gallows?"

"Mr. Bonney, I believe it's common knowledge you violated the terms of the governor's amnesty proclamation. However, that falls outside the purview of this court. Have you anything else to say?"

"No, nothin' that'd interest you."

"William Bonney," the judge intoned, "you have been found guilty of the wanton and premeditated act of murder. It is the judgment of this court that on May 13, 1881, between the hours of sunrise and noon, in the County of Lincoln, New Mexico Territory, you be hanged by the neck until dead. May God have mercy on your soul."

There was a moment of oppressive silence, then Judge Bristol hammered his gavel. "The prisoner is hereby remanded to the custody of the Lincoln County sheriff. This court stands adjourned."

Garrett and Starbuck hustled the Kid out of the courtroom. In the corridor, bypassing the stairs to the jail, they walked directly to a door at the rear of the building. Outside, three mounted deputies waited with a wagon and team. The Kid was unceremoniously lifted into the back of the wagon, and Starbuck scrambled into the driver's seat. Garrett stepped aboard his own mount, and led the way north from Mesilla. Less than sixty seconds had elapsed since the reading of the death warrant.

A short distance outside town, Starbuck glanced around at the Kid. The wagon was loaded with supplies for the three-day ride to Lincoln, and the Kid had made himself comfortable on a pile of bedrolls. He returned Starbuck's look with a disgruntled stare.

"You sure fixed things up with the judge, didn't you?"

"I tried," Starbuck said firmly. "That's all I promised, and I did my best. But he had his mind set."

"Yeah, well," the Kid muttered. "You can forget our deal. Way it looks, you didn't try near hard enough."

"I thought I had your word."

"Hell, my word don't mean do-diddly squat! Besides, I ain't about to help somebody while he's fittin' a noose around my neck."

"Suppose we petition the governor? Would you agree to talk, then?"

"Won't nothin' make me talk except gettin' that death sentence lifted. You arrange it and you've got yourself a witness. You don't, then you might as well crap in one hand and wish in the other."

"You're a hard customer, Billy." Starbuck reflected a moment, then shrugged. "Well, I reckon time's on our side, anyway. We've got a month to make the governor see the light. Might just be enough to turn the trick."

"A month." The Kid gave him a strange crooked smile. "Hell, I hadn't thought about that. Goddamn near anything could happen in a month!"

"You sound awful chipper all of a sudden."

"Well, like the Good Book says, Starbuck: it's always darkest before the dawn. Thirty days and thirty nights, and only the last sunrise counts. Yessir, I like them odds!"

Starbuck merely nodded, and twisted around in his seat. He made a mental note to have a talk with Garrett. Any thought of the governor, or commutation, was now a secondary consideration. The Kid was thinking of those thirty days and thirty nights. And escape.

CHAPTER 12

The door to Garrett's office was locked. Starbuck knocked, waiting a moment, then turned away when there was no response. The county jail, where the Kid was being held, was on the upper floor of the courthouse. He crossed the corridor and mounted the stairs.

Almost two weeks had passed since he and Garrett had delivered the Kid to Lincoln. In that time, he hadn't spoken with the Kid, nor had he communicated any messages through Garrett. Instead, he'd let the young outlaw wonder what was happening, allowing the time to work its own pressure. With each passing day, he knew the uncertainty would have a corrosive effect on the Kid's nerves.

Climbing the stairs, he marveled that their scheme had gone so well. Apparently the Kid still believed they were working on his behalf, trying to secure a commutation of the death sentence. It seemed the only reasonable explanation, for there had been no jailbreak attempts, and according to reports, the Kid was a model prisoner. Yet the truth was poles apart from what the Kid had been led to believe.

There was no chance of commutation. John Chisum had made no overtures toward the governor, and the execution date remained unchanged. On May 13, as scheduled, the Kid would be marched to the gallows.

Biding his time, Starbuck had spent the past ten days at the Jinglebob. Aside from Ellen Nesbeth, whose company he found increasingly pleasant, his thoughts had centered on the Kid. In discussions with Chisum he had explored endless approaches to the final gambit in their plan. The more they talked, the more apparent it became that the simplest approach would also prove the most credible. Privately, Starbuck questioned that anything, short of executive clemency, would persuade the Kid. But he was fully committed to the idea, determined to see it through. And now, walking along the second-floor hallway, he marked once again that the means were always justified when dealing with killers. He steeled himself to lie like a Chinese bandit.

The Lincoln County jail always reminded Starbuck of a circus arena. The lone cell, located in the center of a large room, resembled a wild animal cage. It was essentially a holding pen, constructed of steel bars on the sides and interlaced steel strips on the top. For added security, all other prisoners had been released on bail or transferred to Santa Fe. The Kid had the cell to himself.

Jim Bell and Bob Ollinger, the regular deputies,

were on duty. The night shift, two of Starbuck's men, relieved them every evening at sundown. Bell was an amiable sort, too easygoing in Starbuck's opinion, but nonetheless an efficient officer. Ollinger was his exact opposite, loudmouthed and surly, with a thinly disguised streak of cruelty. Starbuck thought he had all the qualities of a mean dog.

The deputies were seated at a table, playing dominoes, when Starbuck entered the room. Bell rose, greeting him affably. But Ollinger merely looked around, his expression stolid. A double-barrel shotgun, which he always kept close at hand, was propped against the table. Starbuck ignored him, nodding to Bell.

"How's it going?"

"Jim Dandy," Bell said, smiling. "Little boring, but no problems otherwise."

"The Kid's behaving himself, then?"

"Hasn't give us a minute's trouble, and that's a fact."

"Wish to hell he would!"

Ollinger laid the shotgun across his lap. He stared toward the cell, where the Kid was stretched out in a bunk. He patted the shotgun, his voice sullen.

"Scared shitless, ain't you, Billy boy?"

No response.

"Knows he'll get a quart of buckshot up his gizzard if he tries anything funny. Ain't that right, badass? Go on, tell us it ain't so!"

"Ollinger." Starbuck's tone was commanding.

"You and Bell get back to your game. I want to have a word with the Kid."

Ollinger gave him a dirty look, but the baiting subsided. Moving past the table, Starbuck approached the cell. The Kid rolled out of his bunk and walked to the door. His mouth curled in a wide peg-toothed grin.

"Long time no see."

"Billy," Starbuck said pleasantly. "How're things?"

"Awright, except for ol' tough-turd Ollinger. Spends half his day wavin' that scattergun under my nose."

"I wouldn't pay him any attention."

"I don't." The Kid paused, regarding him with a lazy expression. "So where you been keepin' yourself?"

"Santa Fe, mostly," Starbuck lied. "Chisum asked me to sit in on the meetings between the Stockgrowers' Association and the governor."

"Well, don't keep it a secret! What's the news?"

"All bad." Starbuck shook his head, frowning. "The governor won't go for it. He thinks you'd welch on the deal once he commuted your sentence."

"Bullshit!" the Kid exploded. "It worked the other way round last time. He's the one that broke his word, not me!"

Starbuck shrugged. "Maybe he figures tit for tat. At any rate, he says you'll have to show good faith before he'd even consider a deal."

"Good faith?" the Kid repeated. "What the hell's that supposed to mean?"

"A deposition," Starbuck said without expression. "He wants a signed statement with everything you know about Coghlin and Dobson."

"Aww for Chrissakes! He must think I've got mush between my ears. If you had a deposition, then you wouldn't need me!"

"No, you're wrong, Billy. A deposition might get them indicted, but we need you on the witness stand to get a conviction."

"C'mon, Starbuck! That's a crock of applesauce and we both know it."

"I don't follow you."

"Like hell!" The Kid grimaced, flashing a mouthful of brownish teeth. "With a deposition, all you've got to do is wait for me to be hung. Then you bring Dobson and Coghlin to trial, and there ain't no way they could cross-examine a dead man's statement. A jury would convict 'em one, two, three!"

"You're off the mark," Starbuck said earnestly. "A judge wouldn't allow that kind of statement to be entered into evidence. He'd rule it inadmissible, and the jury would never hear it."

"Says you! I got a hunch it'd work just fine. So you trot on back and tell Chisum he can't have his cake and eat it too."

"You care to spell that out?"

"Goddamn, Starbuck, don't play dumb! You aim to let me swing, and you're tryin' to rig it so I'll pull the rest of 'em into the grave with me. Pretty slick thinkin', I'll hand you that. But it ain't gonna work."

"Well, Billy," Starbuck said, watching him carefully, "that sort of puts you between a rock and a hard place. The governor says it's no soap without a deposition, and the way I count, time's running out. You've got fifteen days, and unless you come through, that's all she wrote."

"You lousy bastard!" the Kid raged, glowering at him. "You're worse'n me! You'd sucker a man and then string him up without battin' an eye. You're just mighty goddamn lucky I ain't on the outside. You'd get yours quick, mister! Pronto!"

Starbuck looked solemn. "You've got me wrong, and I'm sorry you feel that way, Billy. I'd advise you to think it over. It's the only chance you've got."

"Don't hold your breath!"

The Kid whirled away, stumping angrily across the cell, and flopped down on his bunk. Starbuck knew then he had lost the game. The outcome brought with it no great surprise; unlike Chisum, who constantly underestimated the opposition, he'd never really believed the Kid would cooperate on the strength of promises alone. But now, having failed, he realized an escape attempt was all the more imminent. With no hope of commutation, the Kid had nothing to lose. A jailbreak was the only alternative to hanging.

Starbuck moved directly to the table, addressing Bell. "Where's Sheriff Garrett?"

"Out collectin' taxes."

"Taxes?"

"Yeah," Bell smiled, bobbing his head, "delinquent taxes. Lots of folks won't pay up till the wolf comes knockin' on their door."

Starbuck hesitated, wondering if he should warn the deputies personally. Then, reluctant to overstep himself further, he decided to wait and speak with Garrett. He nodded absently to Bell, and walked toward the hallway.

On the ground floor, he found the sheriff's office still locked. He pondered a moment, disturbed by the prospect of delay, when Garrett suddenly appeared through the main entrance. After they exchanged greetings, Garrett unlocked his office door and led the way inside.

"Pat," Starbuck said without preliminaries, "we've got big trouble. The Kid's all primed to try a breakout. I'd judge it'll be sometime within the next few days."

"That's what you told me the day we left Mesilla. So far, I haven't seen no indication of it."

"Things have changed," Starbuck noted. "He waited around thinking we might get his sentence commuted. The reason's not important, but he knows different now. He'll make his play for the first chance he gets."

"Maybe he will," Garrett said importantly, "maybe he won't. I'm not especially worried about it one way or the other."

Garrett had taken on grand airs since the Kid's

conviction. Newspaper reporters were hounding him for interviews, and an article in the *Police Gazette* had transformed him into a minor celebrity. Starbuck briefly considered deflating his balloon, then thought better of it. No useful purpose would be served, and it might adversely affect the job at hand.

"Any particular reason," he asked, "why you're not worried?"

"Bob Ollinger," Garrett said, grinning. "He hates the Kid worse'n the devil hates holy water. If the Kid tries to bust out, Bob will dose him with that shotgun and save us the trouble of hangin' him. Either way, though, the Kid winds up in a box. So it's six of one and half a dozen of another."

"If I were you," Starbuck advised, "I'd play it safe. The Kid's tricky as they come, and Ollinger's not exactly a mental wizard."

"Luke, you're a worrywart." Garrett laughed, and slapped him across the shoulder. "You just look after the Nesbeths and leave the Kid to me. Only one way he'll get out of here, and that's feet first."

Outside the courthouse, Starbuck paused to roll a cigarette. His nerves were gritty and restless, and he felt oddly unassured. For all Garrett's confidence, there were still fifteen days until the execution. And the Kid, given the least opportunity, would be long gone before that last sunrise. Yet there was little to be done that hadn't already been done. Somehow, though he couldn't say precisely why, that thought was what worried him the most.

His instinct told him something had been left undone.

Over the next couple of days Starbuck gradually put his mind at ease. The Jinglebob seemed a world apart from Lincoln and the Kid, and he decided it was senseless to brood on things that might—or might not—happen. He rode with Ellen Nesbeth every morning, and after supper, they took walks along the river. She was lively, filled with warmth and spontaneous laughter, and he found himself drawn to her bawdy good humor. More than anything else, she was a pleasant, and very attractive, diversion. She made him forget the Kid.

Then, on his second morning back at the ranch, the outside world once more intruded. Ellen, mounted on a fleet little mare, always insisted that they race the last mile to the corral. A fiery competitor, she considered herself any man's equal on a horse, and she loved to win. Starbuck understood that it was important to her, but he never made allowances for the fact she was a woman. He drove his gelding hard, and forced her to win legitimately, or not at all. Today, running neck and neck, they galloped into the compound in a dead heat. She nosed him out only within the last few yards.

As she dismounted, she was laughing, her eyes bright with excitement. But Starbuck was distracted by one of the hands, who ran forward to meet him. The look on the man's face told him there was trouble, and he prepared himself for the worst. He stepped down from the saddle with a sense of cold fatalism.

"Luke, the old man wants you up at the house!"

"Any idea what it's about?"

"The Kid escaped! Killed a couple of deputies and hightailed it out of Lincoln."

Starbuck excused himself, leaving Ellen looking dazed and suddenly somber. He hurried toward the house, aware he'd forgotten to ask which deputies had been killed. His pace quickened.

Some moments later he entered the study. Chisum was seated in his usual chair, and turned as he came through the door. One of his own men, Frank Miller, rose from the other chair. He breathed a sigh of relief, ignoring Miller's hangdog expression. He halted, his eyes hard.

"What happened?"

"The Kid busted out. Killed Bell and Ollinger."

"How?"

Miller told a fragmented story. Yesterday at noon Ollinger had stepped across the street for dinner. Somehow, though it was still a mystery, the Kid had managed to get hold of Bell's pistol. When Bell made a break for the stairs, the Kid shot and killed him. Upon hearing gunfire, Ollinger left his meal and started back across the street. The Kid, perched in an upstairs window of the courthouse, called out to him. Ollinger glanced up to find himself staring into the muzzle of his own shotgun. Onlookers said the Kid laughed, and then gave Ollinger both barrels in the chest. Terrified, the witnesses to the shooting scattered and took cover. The Kid, by then heavily armed, calmly left the courthouse and commandeered a horse. He rode out of Lincoln unchallenged.

"Me and Cole," Miller concluded, "was asleep at the hotel. We didn't hear the shootin', and it all happened so fast, nobody thought to come get us. By the time we was woke up, it was too late. The Kid had skedaddled."

"Where was Garrett?"

"Out collectin' taxes." Miller paused, studying the floor. "He's broke up bad, Luke. Took it real hard. He told me to hump it, and get you back to town straightaway."

A quietness fell over Starbuck. He dismissed Miller, who had ridden all night, ordering him to get some rest. When the door closed, he turned slowly to Chisum. His features were grim, and his mouth was set in a thin line.

"I'll leave soon as I get my gear together."

"Sorry, Luke." Chisum's expression was downcast. "I know that ain't much consolation, what with you havin' to start all over from scratch." He shifted uncomfortably in his chair. "Anything I can do to help?"

"One thing," Starbuck told him. "I'm taking John Poe with me, but I'll leave the rest of the boys here to guard the Nesbeths. They'll have their orders, so I'd appreciate it if you wouldn't get in their way."

"Hell, Luke, that ain't necessary! Go on and take

them boys along; you might need 'em. We'll look after the Nesbeths just fine."

"No," Starbuck said flatly. "I'm the one that got the Nesbeths behind the eight ball, and with the Kid loose, it makes things worse. From here on out, I want my own men on the job."

Chisum lifted an eyebrow in question. "Why would the Kid make a try for the Nesbeths?"

"He won't," Starbuck countered. "But Coghlin and his bunch might get some bright ideas. They'd like nothing better than to do away with the Nesbeths and let everybody blame it on the Kid. That way they'd be off the hook all the way round."

"Yeah," Chisum said, troubled, "you've got a point there. Specially since they'll know you're off huntin' the Kid."

Starbuck eyed him a moment, considering. "I reckon you ought to know something. I aim to get the Kid and I aim to keep the Nesbeths alive, but that's all. From now on anything else is your lookout. I don't want nothing more to do with your politics."

"You're sore 'cause the Kid got away, ain't you?"

"No, John, I'm not sore. I'm plumb pissed off."

Starbuck turned and crossed the study. He opened the door, moving into the hallway, and closed it behind him. The chime of his spurs slowly faded as he walked from the house.

An hour later, with Poe at his side, he rode toward Lincoln.

CHAPTER 13

There was a light in Garrett's office. Farther down the street, a crowd of men were gathered outside the largest of the town's saloons. The sound of loud talk and drunken laughter was intensified by the late-night stillness.

Starbuck and Poe reined to a halt before the courthouse. The commotion outside the saloon, un-usual at any time in Lincoln, held their attention. They sat for a moment, listening and watching, struck by the raucous tone of the crowd. Though neither of them spoke, they exchanged a puzzled glance. With the Kid escaped, and two lawmen dead, there seemed little for the townspeople to cel-ebrate. Finally, somewhat at a loss, they dismounted and tied their horses to the hitch rack.

John Poe slapped trail dust off his clothes, and fell in beside Starbuck. They had ridden straight through from the Jinglebob, scarcely talking the en-tire time. He took Starbuck's quiet mood as an om-inous sign, much like a thunderhead darkening the skies before a storm. All the way into town one thought kept recurring, and now, as they walked toward the courthouse steps, he silently underscored the sentiment to himself. He was quite happy not to be standing in Pat Garrett's boots. Not tonight.

When they entered the office, Garrett looked up from behind his desk. He was hunched over a territorial map, unfurled across the desk top, and his features appeared haggard in the glow of lamplight. He rose, smiling weakly, and extended his hand.

"Been expectin' you, Luke. You made good time."

"Not good enough." Starbuck pointedly ignored the handshake. "I'd say we're about a day late, wouldn't you, Pat?"

Garrett flushed, quickly dropped his hand. "Awright, goddammit, you was right and I was wrong. You told me and I should've listened to you, and I wish to hell I had. So just don't rub it in, Luke! I've been kickin' my ass ever since it happened."

"Tell me about that," Starbuck said with a flat stare. "Miller wasn't too clear on details. Exactly how'd it happen?"

"Well, it's only a guess, but I've got an idea the Kid talked Bell into takin' him to the privy. He'd come down with a case of the trots—"

"The trots!" Starbuck interrupted. "He looked plenty healthy when I was here the day before."

"Yeah, I know," Garrett said glumly. "Course, hindsight's no better than hind tit."

"So he faked it and got Bell to let him out of the lockup to go to the outhouse. Then what?"

"Why, he must've jumped Bell somehow. He had

146

it planned out pretty slick, the way he waited till Ollinger went to dinner. So Bell got careless, what with the Kid bellyachin' and carrying on. It all fits."

"And nobody—" Starbuck paused, a knot throbbing in his jaw. "He just rode out of town and nobody lifted a finger to stop him."

"Not then," Garrett said defensively. "Hell, everyone that seen it like to wet their drawers. He damn near blew Bob Ollinger half in two with that scattergun!"

Starbuck squinted, watching him. "What do you mean, 'Not then'? That sounds like things have changed somehow."

"I'll say they have!" Garrett crowed, squaring his shoulders. "I put out a call for a posse and just about had to beat 'em off with a switch. Every sonovabitch and his dog volunteered!"

"A posse." Starbuck looked genuinely surprised. "You're talking about that bunch down at the saloon, aren't you?"

"Yep!" Garrett beamed, thumbs hooked in his vest. "Took the pick of the litter! Twenty men, already sworn in and ready to ride at daylight."

"Twenty drunks would be more like it. In case you haven't checked lately, they're tanked up on rotgut and going strong."

"Oh, don't pay that no nevermind. A couple of hours in the saddle and they'll sober up quick enough."

"What's holding you?" Starbuck asked. "You've had since yesterday noon to take the trail."

"Why, hell, Luke!" Garrett said affably. "I was waitin' on you to get here. Wouldn't hardly seem fair to go off without you."

"Then I reckon you just wasted a day."

"Wasted—" Garrett stopped, no longer grinning. "I don't get it."

"You'll have to handle this one by yourself, Pat. I don't care much for crowds, and I damn sure don't want any part of a wild-goose chase."

"C'mon, now, you got no call to say that."

"No?" Starbuck studied him a moment, frowning. "You take a posse out and you might as well telegraph ahead and let the Kid know you're coming. I'd rate your chances of catching him at about zero. Maybe less."

"I suppose you know a better way?"

"Yeah," Starbuck nodded, "I do. A couple of men, working real quiet, could run him down before he ever got wind they were tracking him."

"Lemme guess," Garrett said sourly. "You had yourself and Poe in mind, didn't you? I sit here on my thumb, and you two take off on your lonesome. Wasn't that about the size of it?"

"You want the Kid, don't you?"

"Hell, yes!" Garrett flared. "But the Kid's only part of it! Him breakin' jail made me look like a fool. So I've got to make a show of huntin' him down. A damn big show! Otherwise, I'm in a heap of trouble."

"And if I'm right?" Starbuck demanded. "If it turns out to be a wild-goose chase? What then?"

"I can't let that happen, Luke. I've got to catch him—got to, goddammit!—or else I'm a dead duck come election time."

Starbuck was silent for a long while. At last, with a look of weary resignation, he shrugged. "Where did you aim to start?"

Garrett turned the map on the desk. Starbuck and Poe moved closer, and he began a quick explanation of the search he'd planned. His finger traced a path west through the mountains, then across the Carrizozo Plains and along the slopes of the Oscuros. From there, he indicated the Three Rivers country, then the Organ Mountains, and, finally, a sweep through the border. When he finished, he stood back, awaiting Starbuck's verdict.

"That pretty well covers it," Starbuck allowed, "except for Fort Sumner."

"Oh, hell, Luke, he'd never go back there. Not in a month of Sundays! The Kid's too smart for that."

"Well, it's your show, Pat. You run it whichever way suits you best. I'll leave Poe with you—"

"Hold on! You mean you're not comin' along?"

"No." Starbuck shook his head. "You don't need me. I'll just stick close to the Jinglebob and keep an eye on the Nesbeths. Wouldn't pay to take any more chances with them."

Garrett looked relieved. "I suspect you're right, Luke. Makes damn good sense all the way round."

Starbuck purposely avoided any further discussion. He noted it had been a long day, commenting

149

he would spend the night at the hotel, and left the office. Poe, after agreeing to meet Garrett and the posse at dawn, went along. Outside, walking toward their horses, Starbuck appeared thoughtful. When the silence held, Poe's curiosity finally got the better of him.

"You really headed back to the Jinglebob," he asked quietly, "or have you got some notion of trailin' the Kid on your own?"

"I considered that," Starbuck admitted, "but it'd just be wasted effort. I figure the Kid will stay on the move, leastways till Garrett gets tired of chasing around the territory. If I was him, I wouldn't spend two nights running in the same place."

"What's the sense in me taggin' along with Garrett, then?"

"Hold his hand," Starbuck remarked. "Keep him from making too big a fool of himself. He'll call it quits soon enough, and once the dust settles, that's when we'll make our move."

"How you aim to go about it?"

Starbuck smiled. "I'll be thinking on it, John. There's ways and there's ways, and it'll come to me by the time the Kid goes to roost. You just let me know when Garrett's got his fill."

Poe merely nodded. He was accustomed to Starbuck's cryptic manner, and as they mounted their horses and rode toward the livery stable, he knew he'd been told the one thing that mattered. Sometime soon, quietly and on his own, Starbuck meant to stalk the Kid and kill him. No quarter asked, none given.

Across town, in the home of Judge Owen Hough, another meeting was under way. Jack Dobson and Joe Coghlin were seated in the study. The sliding doors were closed, and the judge sat behind a walnut desk, assessing the two men with a cool look. His features were immobile, revealing nothing.

Since January, the strategy outlined by Warren Mitchell had proved almost infallible. Their monthly meetings were amicable, and according to Mitchell, their associates in Santa Fe were pleased by the gradual progression of affairs. John Chisum's health continued to deteriorate, and there was every reason to believe he wouldn't last out the year. The kid had been convicted and sentenced, and exactly as predicted, he hadn't cooperated with the authorities. The single fly in the ointment was the range detective, Luke Starbuck. Somehow, possibly through the Kid, he had uncovered information of an incriminating nature. In turn, he'd been led to Coghlin's ranch and the Nesbeths, and had developed what appeared to be a fairly strong circumstantial case. Still, despite all he'd learned, no charges had been filed. Which meant the Nesbeths were being held in reserve until some future time. The threat, then, was real, though hardly insurmountable. Witnesses were of no value unless they lived to testify.

For his part, Owen Hough had earned the praise of the men in Santa Fe. By one device or another, he had kept Dobson and Coghlin in line, and no hint of the political ramifications had been allowed to surface. He had the Lincoln operation under control and proceeding smoothly on schedule.

Then, yesterday at noon, all that had changed. With the Kid's escape, Hough was suddenly forced to assume full responsibility for the Pecos Valley venture. There was no way he could safely telegraph Warren Mitchell for instructions, and their next meeting was not scheduled until the latter part of the month. The situation dictated immediate action, and there was nowhere he could turn for advice. He was on his own.

The problem was compounded by Dobson and Coghlin. Their nerves were of the caliber he associated with small-time grifters; they lacked the strength of character necessary to a time of adversity. Watching them now, he knew tonight's meeting represented a critical juncture. Unless he calmed their fears, and somehow restored their confidence, they might very well crack under pressure. Which would spell disaster for him as well.

His voice dispassionate, he addressed them with a look of easy candor. "Gentlemen, let me assure you there's no cause for alarm. Even with the sheriff out of town, William Bonney wouldn't dare set foot in Lincoln."

"What's to stop him?" Coghlin insisted. "Once Garrett and that posse are gone, he could ride in here and do anything he damn well pleased."

"Perhaps," Hough conceded. "But believe me, he won't. You're assuming he has some grudge to settle, and that simply isn't the case."

"I don't agree," Dobson said nervously. "Granted, we got him a change of venue and all that. But I'm convinced he expected something more from us."

"Such as?"

"God only knows! The Kid's crazy as a loon! He probably thought we'd spring him somehow, maybe a commutation. Why else would he wait till two weeks before the hanging to bust out? He sure as hell didn't stick around because he liked jail cooking."

"Perhaps yesterday was the first opportunity he had. You're reading a great deal into it, Jack. I daresay, much more than exists."

"I know the Kid," Dobson countered, "and you don't! He's a vengeful little backshooter, and I'd bet money he thinks we sold him down the river. I told you all along we weren't doing enough! Not to his way of thinking, anyhow."

"Anything more was impossible," Hough said firmly. "We couldn't risk being connected to a common murderer, not this late in the game."

"We?" Dobson echoed. "Hell, it's not we you're talking about. It's that bunch in Santa Fe! The whole idea was to protect their hides, and no way on God's green earth you'll ever convince me otherwise."

"Yeah," Coghlin muttered. "We told you from the start what the Kid was like. You should've listened to us, judge! If we'd only fooled him into believing we was tryin' to help out, then none of this would've happened."

Hough brushed aside the objection. "I don't care to argue the matter any further. You two have your minds made up, so we'll let it rest there. But I direct your attention to certain advantages you've quite obviously overlooked. Has it ever occurred to you that we've been handed a remarkable opportunity?"

Dobson and Coghlin exchanged a quizzical look. When neither of them replied, he went on. "I refer to the fact that Pat Garrett is the laughingstock of Lincoln County. Unless he redeems himself, then he's through in politics. And that, gentlemen, means he will not attempt to recapture Mr. Bonney."

"What?" Dobson scowled. "What the hell are you saying, Owen?"

"I'm saying"—Hough paused for effect, "Garrett will kill the Kid. He needs something to capture the public's imagination, and nothing does it like a shootout. You can take my word on it—the Kid's as good as dead."

"Christ!" Coghlin mumbled. "Wouldn't that be sweet? It'd sure get us off the hook, wouldn't it?"

"It would indeed," Hough said, smiling. "But only halfway, I'm afraid."

Dobson gave him an odd look. "Now you're talking about the Nesbeths, aren't you?"

"Very perceptive, Jack. And, of course, you're

right. We have a chance to wipe the slate clean. No links to the past and nothing to hinder our plans for the future."

"I don't get it," Coughlin said, glancing from one to the other. "What's the big deal about killin' them now?"

"The big deal," Dobson informed him, "is that the Kid's on the loose. Isn't that what you had in mind, judge?"

"Precisely," Hough nodded. "The timing couldn't be more perfect. Chisum and his crowd will naturally jump to the conclusion that the Kid killed them. We couldn't ask for a better opportunity."

"Two birds with one stone," Coghlin laughed. "The Kid gets the Nesbeths, and Garrett gets the Kid. Goddamn!"

"There's one problem," Hough added. "We have to get the Nesbeths before Garrett gets the Kid. Otherwise it won't work."

"Why, hell," Coghlin grunted, "that's simple enough. I'll just tell Gantry to get on it muy pronto. The way he feels about the Nesbeths, he'd count it a pleasure."

There was a long moment of silence. Owen Hough studied the men across from him with a speculative gaze. Then, almost as though thinking aloud, he spoke directly to Coghlin.

"Tell him not to miss. I have a feeling we won't get a second chance."

CHAPTER 14

In the dark, fireflies darted among the trees. Starbuck and the girl were seated under a willowy cottonwood, talking quietly. Their voices were muted by the purl of the river, and they were only dimly visible beneath the moonless sky. She was close enough to touch, and her nearness seemed to him an invitation. She smelled sweet and alluring.

These evening walks had become something of a ritual. Following supper, whenever Starbuck was at the ranch, they excused themselves early and strolled off toward their favorite spot overlooking the river. Understandably, though the matter had never been discussed openly, everyone assumed they were lovers. Sallie Chisum, scarcely civil at times, made no effort to hide her disgust. Her father, who thought she was secretly jealous, looked on the whole affair with rueful good humor. The Nesbeths, on the other hand, knew their daughter and therefore surmised the worst. They accepted, as a matter of form, that she had seduced Starbuck. Their attitude was one of humiliation and shame, and disgruntled silence.

Starbuck, oddly enough, hadn't laid a hand on the girl. He was a confirmed womanizer, with all the instincts of a randy tomcat. His string of conquests included several ranchers' daughters—none of whom had gotten him anywhere near an altar—and he was on intimate terms with dance hall girls in every cowtown within riding distance of the Panhandle. Yet his feelings about Ellen Nesbeth veered wildly.

Over the past few months, the safety of the Jinglebob had brought about a marked change in her attitude. As her fears diminished, the friction between them dwindled as well, and she gradually warmed to Starbuck. Whenever they were together she seemed poised for laughter, filled with verve and gaiety. She no longer treated him like an unwanted protector; her manner was flirtatious and teasing, and she gave the impression an advance would not be unwelcome. Still, though the temptation was difficult to resist, he had kept her at arm's length. He was wary of involvement, fearful her parents would believe he had betrayed a trust, and taken advantage of the situation. Then too, he genuinely liked the girl, and found himself reluctant to test the depth of his own emotions. He avoided physical contact, and tried to ignore her broader hints. He also slept badly.

Tonight, evidencing a new vein of curiosity, she had turned the conversation to his personal life. Under normal circumstances, her questions would have been met with blunt reserve. But he was distracted by thoughts of Garrett—whose search for the Kid had begun only three days ago—and her opening question had caught him off guard. He was uncomfortable talking about himself, but there seemed no easy way to change the subject. For her part, Ellen was playfully amused by his discomfort. She was intrigued as well by that part of himself he kept hidden.

"Do you like your job?" she asked pleasantly. "I mean . . . well, you know . . . most people think a range detective doesn't do anything but go around hanging cow thieves."

"I've never put much store in what people think."

"It doesn't bother you, then—hanging men?"

"Some," Starbuck admitted. "But I've never hung a man that wasn't caught red-handed. Unless I had the goods on them, then they got off with a warning to stay clear of the Panhandle."

She looked at him with impudent eyes. "That's a little like playing God, isn't it?"

"Maybe." Starbuck was gruffly defensive. "Somebody's got to do it, though. Otherwise nothing would be safe, including a man's home and family. I suppose it's all a matter of where you draw the line."

"How many men have you hung?"

"God A'mighty! Hasn't anyone ever told you there are some questions you just don't ask?"

She cocked her head in a funny little smile. "They say you have killed a dozen men in gunfights, maybe more."

"Who says?"

"People," she said mischievously. "Everyone on the Jinglebob gossips about you. To hear them talk, you're sort of a cross between Wild Bill Hickok and a man-eating tiger."

"Well—" Starbuck broke off, chuckling softly. "You sure got yourself an earful, didn't you?"

"Nooo," she said slowly. "I only heard enough to make me curious."

"Oh, how so?"

She searched his face in the dim starlight. "If you like your work so much, why haven't you become a peace officer? Wouldn't a badge make the job easier?"

"Chisum made a good argument for that the day I rode in here. So I listened to him and agreed to let Garrett deputize me. The way it turned out, it made things tougher, not easier."

"I don't understand."

Starbuck pondered a moment. "You remember the fellow I told you about, Ben Langham?" She nodded and he went on. "The Kid killed him and there's no whichaway about it. If I hadn't been wearing a star, we would've hung him when we caught him. But we went by the book—played it straight and gave him his day in court—and you see what happened. He's loose and we're right back where we started."

"Are you saying he shouldn't have had a trial?"

"I'm saying all the legal delays kept him alive past his time. As a result, he's killed two more men and escaped and Christ Himself couldn't guarantee where it'll end."

"Would you have hung them all? Coghlin and Dobson and Gantry, all without a trial?"

"Every last one," Starbuck said gravely. "They're accessories to murder, and except for them, none of this would've happened. I figure they deserve whatever they get, and the faster the better."

"I couldn't agree more! But isn't that for a jury to decide? I mean, after all, that's why we have laws, isn't it?"

"Justice and the law aren't always the same thing. There's times when a man has to choose between them in order to get the job done."

"The terrible swift sword, with no legal tomfoolery?"

"It's a damnsight more certain than the courts! Especially for people like the Kid."

A hot rush of awareness swept over Ellen. Something in the timbre of his voice—the danger and deadly intensity of the man—evoked responses that left her weak in the knees and short of breath. She was drawn to him in some way she couldn't define, and each time they were together her fascination became all the more compelling. Yet she warned herself to beware of any emotional attachment. Behind that hard exterior was a hard man, and if not altogether insensitive, he nonetheless displayed little tolerance for weakness in others. She wanted him, but she felt very much like a small girl playing with matches. She told herself to go slow and hold to a light vein, for she sensed there was nothing beyond the moment, no tomorrow. Abruptly, heeding her own advice, she switched topics with a disingenuous air and a fetching smile.

"Why is it you have never married?"

Starbuck looked at her with some surprise. "Wrong line of work, I guess. Fellow in my trade doesn't run across many women who want to jump the broom with him."

"Fiddlesticks!" she said brightly. "Sallie Chisum is so sweet on you she goes tongue-tied every time you walk into the room."

"You're pulling my leg."

"I certainly am not!" Her throaty laughter floated across the still night. "All you need to do is snap your fingers! Sallie would jump the broom, and the old man would hand you the Jinglebob on a silver platter."

"No, you're wrong," Starbuck said in a low voice. "Even if you weren't, that'd be a poor reason to marry somebody."

"Poor, my eye! The Jinglebob will make someone a very handsome wedding present. Are you sure you won't think it over, Luke? You could do lots worse."

"Wouldn't doubt it. But don't you see, it'd just be another headache on top of the old one."

"What would?"

"The Jinglebob."

"What are you talking about?"

"My ranch."

"Your ranch!" She stared at him, astounded. "You own a ranch?"

"Yeah," Starbuck said, not cracking a smile. "The LX, over in the Panhandle. Course, it's only about half the size of the Jinglebob, but it's a nice little spread."

"You—!" She tossed her head, pouting. "You just let me run on and make a fool of myself. That's cruel."

"I didn't hardly see any way to stop you."

She sniffed. "It's probably a big fib, anyhow! Are you sure you own a ranch?"

"Cross my heart."

"And it's really half the size of the Jinglebob?"

"Close enough, give or take a few thousand acres."

She eyed him suspiciously. "Where did a range detective get an outfit that big?"

Starbuck looked away, suddenly somber. "Ben Langham willed it to me."

"The man the Kid—?"

"Yeah," Starbuck said quietly. "You might say the Kid made me a rich man."

"Oh, Luke." She touched his arm. "I'm sorry, I had no idea . . ."

Her voice trailed off. The warmth of her hand triggered something within him. All restraint dispelled, he took her in his arms. Whatever he'd guessed about her past, he was not prepared for the depth of her ardor, her sensual eagerness. Her lips were moist and inviting, and she greedily darted his mouth with her tongue. Her arms circled his neck with desperate urgency, and she pulled him down on the ground. He stretched out beside her on the grassy riverbank, and she snuggled closer, moaning softly. Her breasts were firm and swollen, her nipples pressed hard through his shirt, and he felt himself growing aroused by the feverish movement of her hips. His hand slipped beneath her skirt, touched yielding flesh, then quickly moved upward, caressing the warmth of her thigh. She began to tremble, her body wracked by convulsions, and her legs parted. Her nails dug into his shoulders, fierce talons holding him tighter, and he rolled on top of her. One hand clutching her buttocks, he began fumbling with the buttons on his pants. Her legs went around him, urging him.

A gunshot split the night. Too quick to count, the roar of a rifle hammered out several more shots in a staccato burst.

Starbuck scrambled to his feet. Cursing savagely, he ordered her not to move, and hurried off into the darkness. Once clear of the trees, he sprinted hard, running toward the main house. Ahead, he heard shouting and saw dim figures dashing across the compound. He flipped the leather thong off the hammer of his Colt, jerking and cocking the pistol in one smooth motion. His stride lengthened to a dead lope.

Outside the house, a clot of men stood jammed together before the veranda. Their voices swelled in a confused murmur, and several cowhands toward the front seemed to be shouting questions. Then the door opened and a spill of lamplight flooded the yard. John Chisum, with his daughter at his side, hobbled across the veranda.

Starbuck bulled a path through the crowd. He saw one of his own men, Jessie Tuttle, separate from the cowhands and approach the veranda. He recalled Tuttle had pulled the early watch tonight, guarding the perimeter of the house, and he grasped the situation immediately. It was Tuttle, still carrying his saddle carbine, who had fired the shots.

Chisum spotted him as he moved into the silty glow of lamplight. Tuttle turned, nodding soberly, and he halted before them. He felt Sallie Chisum's eyes on him, but he directed his attention to Tuttle.

"Let's have it, Jessie," he said, catching his breath from the run. "What happened?"

"Three men," Tuttle replied crisply, "maybe four. Sorta hard to tell in the dark. I was posted out back of the house and—well, you know how it is at night—all I caught was movement, more like shadows than anything else. I sung out real loud, and they took off like scalded dogs. That's when I cut loose."

"You were the only one that fired?"

"Yep," Tuttle grinned. "I sprayed 'em good! Black as pitch out there, so I just let go and hoped I'd get lucky."

"Any idea what they had in mind?"

"Not rightly. But the way they was headed put 'em on a beeline for the Nesbeths' bedroom window. I reckoned that was reason enough to stop 'em right where they was."

"You reckoned right," Starbuck acknowledged. "Any chance you winged one of them?"

"Nope," Tuttle said bitterly. "I heard a bunch of horses all take off at once. Figures they would've been slowed down some if anybody had caught a slug."

"Where were the horses, which direction?"

"North, over by that stand of trees where the crick runs into the river. Good hunnert yards away, but they made it lickety-split when I started dustin' their heels."

"Get some lanterns," Starbuck ordered, jerking a thumb at the throng of cowhands. "Take these boys and search that area foot by foot. If you spot any blood sign, give me a yell real quick."

The men trooped off into the night, and Starbuck quickly assessed the situation. Someone, intent on killing the Nesbeths, had been thwarted only at the last moment. A worm of doubt gnawed at him as he considered moving the Nesbeths to a safer location. Then, with bleak irony, he reminded himself there was no place safer than the Jinglebob. It would be necessary to double the guard and maintain constant vigilance. And he saw, too, that he could no longer afford to wait on Garrett. His own plan, complicated further by tonight's attack, must be put into effect without delay. At length, he turned to Chisum.

"I'm going after the Kid first thing tomorrow."

"Alone?"

"Alone," Starbuck told him. "We're running short on time, and one way or another, it's got to end."

"This business tonight," Chisum asked tentatively, "you think it was the Kid?"

"Maybe," Starbuck said without conviction. "Or maybe somebody that wanted us to think it was the Kid. Either way, it won't be settled until he's hung out to dry."

"Then you intend to kill him?"

Starbuck's eyes were angry, commanding. "Just as sure as God made little green apples."

Sallie Chisum suddenly drew a sharp breath. She stared past him a mere instant, then wheeled around, skirts flying, and marched into the house. He turned and saw Ellen walking toward them. Her clothes were disheveled and a long strand of hair hung loose on her neck. She stopped, her gaze fixed on him with a look of dulled terror.

"Were my folks . . . hurt?"

"No, they're fine." He gently touched her arm. "Why don't you go tell them there's nothing to worry about? I'll come by when I get things squared away."

She nodded, glancing absently at Chisum, and crossed the veranda. There was a moment of silence until she went through the door and disappeared down the hallway. Then Chisum grunted, his mouth curled in a wry smile.

"You'll likely find it a mite safer off huntin' the

Kid. There's gonna be lots of fireworks around here after tonight."

"Jesus!" Starbuck muttered. "Women sure do complicate things."

"Why, son, you ain't seen the half of it! Wait'll the fight really starts!"

Starbuck shook his head, and walked off toward the creek. Watching him, Chisum was struck by a whimsical notion, and suddenly chuckled. He wondered how it felt to be a manhunter and a lady-killer—all rolled into one!

CHAPTER 15

Starbuck's disguise was convincing though not elaborate. A brushy mustache covered his upper lip and a carefully cultivated stubble shadowed his features from chin to jawbone. He looked grimy and trail-worn, and his clothes were a regular rainbow of foul odors. Which was a normal condition for any man who rode the owlhoot. After a close inspection, even a diehard skeptic found it easy to believe he was only one step ahead of the law.

For the past two months, he had scoured the better part of New Mexico Territory. His route was roughly opposite to the path taken by Pat Garrett, who had long since abandoned the search and retired to Lincoln to await word of the Kid's whereabouts. On the move constantly, he had begun the hunt along the border. A week of discreet inquiry, pausing briefly in villages on both sides of the line, left him convinced the Kid had not sought refuge in Old Mexico. From there he had turned north, criss-crossing back and forth on wide sweeps that covered the central half of the territory. Every couple of weeks he returned to the Jinglebob, stopping overnight to exchange information with Chisum. Then, expecting no word of the Kid and receiving none, he quickly resumed the search. He drifted from towns to outlying ranches to rugged mountainous camps. And he found nothing.

At the outset, his plan had been based on a simple premise. He believed, with some conviction, that the Kid would go to ground once Garrett called it quits and stopped chasing around the countryside. Long ago he had mastered the trick common to game hunters: a man who consistently put meat on the table learned to think like his prey. In the Kid's place, he would have avoided Garrett's posse, then retreated to a secure hideout and laid low until the furor subsided. Yet it was not enough for a manhunter to merely think like an outlaw. Much the same as a wilderness hunter, he used that knowledge to cut sign and shorten the chase, and ultimately bring his quarry to bay. To date, the Kid had left no spoor, not the slightest trace.

Starbuck's cover story, like his physical disguise, was a work of credible simplicity. He posed as a friend of Dave Rudabaugh's, one of the outlaws captured at Stinking Springs with the Kid. Along with the rest of the gang, Rudabaugh had been convicted on a variety of charges and sentenced to a long term in prison. After exhausting all appeals, the conviction had been upheld and the gang members were to be transferred from the Santa Fe jail to federal prison on July 15. By weaving known fact with plausible invention, Starbuck was able to fab-

ricate a tale that had the ring of truth. Dave Rudabaugh had put out a call for help, requesting that
the Kid arrange a jailbreak before the gang was
transferred to federal prison. Passing himself off
as a go-between, Starbuck told the same story
everywhere he went. He desperately needed to make
contact with the Kid, and deliver Rudabaugh's message. Otherwise the men who had loyally stuck by
El Chivato would spend the rest of their days on a
federal rockpile.

His tale drew sympathy from bartenders and
wide-eyed peons and an assortment of hardcases
who frequented back alley cantinas all across the
territory. But no leads surfaced, and the trail proved
cold as a demon winter wind. To all intents and
purposes, the Kid had disappeared from the face of
the earth.

At last, on the morning of July 10, Starbuck admitted he'd reached an impasse. His quest had con-
sumed two wearying months and taken him on a
corkscrew odyssey of nearly a thousand miles. Always on guard, constantly in the saddle, his bones
ached as though he'd been run through an ore
crusher. Even worse, the long, futile weeks of
searching had sapped his will, left him emotionally
drained. He saw no reason to punish himself further.

Outside Santa Fe, he paused at a crossroads. To
the south lay Lincoln and the Jinglebob, and an end
to a grueling journey. But with that end, having
come full circle, he would be forced to swallow the
bitter pill of defeat. It grated on him to think he'd

fared no better than Pat Garrett. A matter of professional pride was involved, and he suddenly cursed himself as a quitter.

His gaze turned east, along a road that crossed the Manzano Mountains and led ultimately to Fort Sumner. There was little to be gained in that direction; he believed, like Garrett, that the Kid would avoid old haunts and known friends. Still, it was the one spot he hadn't covered, and perhaps his last chance to unearth a lead. Pete Maxwell, the rancher headquartered there, was a staunch defender of the Kid, and a longtime friend. While the odds dictated otherwise, it was always possible he'd heard from the Kid, or at least had some knowledge as to the outlaw's general whereabouts. If there was nothing to be gained in talking with Maxwell, there was certainly nothing to be lost.

Starbuck reined his horse eastward, toward Fort Sumner. He told himself it was just slightly out of the way, and therefore no real waste of time. And it delayed, if only by a day, his inevitable return to the Jinglebob.

Shortly after noontime the next day, Starbuck dismounted before Maxwell's house. He left his horse ground-reined and proceeded up the stone walkway. A middle-aged man with dark hair and a bulge around his beltline stepped through the door. He moved to the edge of the porch and stood digging at his teeth with a toothpick as Starbuck approached. His expression was neutral.

"Howdy."

"Afternoon," Starbuck responded. "Hope I didn't interrupt your dinner."

"No, I just now got up from the table. What can I do for you?"

"Thought maybe you could point me in the direction of Pete Maxwell."

"Who might you be?"

"Name's Bob Brown," Starbuck said in a weary tone. "I've got a message for Maxwell."

"No need to look no further, Mr. Brown. I'm Pete Maxwell."

"Then you'd know the feller that sent me, Dave Rudabaugh."

Maxwell stopped picking his teeth. "Yeah, I used to be on speakin' terms with Rudabaugh."

"I reckon you heard him and the rest of the boys pulled a long stretch?"

"Word gets around."

"Maybe you heard they're gonna be shipped off to the federal pen come next Monday?"

"Suppose I had?" Maxwell said, frowning. "What's that got to do with me?"

"Dave needs help." Starbuck took out the makings and sprinkled tobacco into a rolling paper. "He ain't exactly hankerin' to take that trip."

"I wouldn't be surprised."

Starbuck licked, sealing the paper, and twisted the ends. He struck a match, glancing up at Maxwell as he lit the cigarette. "Dave figures to bust out of jail. But he's gonna need someone on the outside to lend a hand."

"That a fact?" Maxwell studied him a moment. "You sayin' he had some idea I'd help spring him?"

"Nope," Starbuck said, exhaling a thin streamer of smoke. "But he thought you might get word to the Kid. He figures Bonney owes him one, for old-times' sake."

"Bob Brown." Maxwell underscored the words with a slow drawl. "I don't recall hearin' that name before. Who're you to Dave Rudabaugh?"

"A friend." Starbuck met his look squarely. "Let's get something straight, Mr. Maxwell. Dave got me out of a scrape once and I'm returnin' the favor. But I'm just a messenger boy in this here deal, nothin' more. I quit the owlhoot a long time ago, and I don't aim to get bollixed up in no jail-break."

"Ain't likely you will," Maxwell said coolly. "The way things stack up, you rode out here for nothin'."

"How so?"

"The Kid lit out for Mexico when he busted jail. Last I heard, he was holed up somewheres down in Sonora."

"Sonora!" Starbuck appeared distressed, took a couple of quick puffs on his cigarette. "Jesus, that don't give me much time! Any idea where I might find him?"

"Even if I knew—which I don't—it wouldn't do

no good. You only got four days till Rudabaugh's shipped out, and it'd take you damn near that long to locate the Kid. You might as well ride on back and tell Rudabaugh it just didn't pan out."

"Yeah," Starbuck grunted, "luck of the draw, ain't it?"

"Wish I could've been more help. Tell Rudabaugh and the rest of the boys I was askin' after them."

"I'll do that, Mr. Maxwell. Much obliged for your time."

Starbuck turned and plodded wearily back to his horse. He wasn't at all sure Maxwell had told him the truth; but there was no sign of tension, and no reason to believe the rancher knew anything of value. Then too, it was entirely possible the Kid had avoided the border towns and crossed into Mexico without leaving a trace. He ground his cigarette into the dirt, suddenly disgusted. *To hell with it!*

Pete Maxwell stood sucking on his toothpick. He watched Starbuck mount and ride west from the settlement. Only when horse and rider were dimly visible in the distance did he turn away. He entered the house and stopped just inside a bedroom which overlooked the veranda.

The Kid was positioned beside a window. His gaze was fixed on the western road, and a moment elapsed before he glanced around. His expression was grim.

"What do you think?" Maxwell asked. "Was he on the level?"

"Pete, it's a damn good thing you've got a poker face. The jasper you been talkin' with was Luke Starbuck."

"Starbuck!" Maxwell parroted. "The range detective?"

"Big as life." The Kid scowled, shook his head. "Sonovabitch just don't give up! I wasn't never worried about Garrett, but I was sure as hell hopin' we'd seen the last of that hardass."

"You think he bought my story?"

"Sounded like it." The Kid paused, considering. "Course, that ain't no guarantee he won't be back. I got a hunch it's time to be movin' on."

"Mexico?"

"Why not?" The Kid shrugged, a hint of mockery in his eyes. "Somewheres down around Sonora, wasn't that what you said?"

"You'll need money," Maxwell noted somberly. "I only got a couple of hundred here in the house, but I could send along some more later."

"No, you done too much already, Pete. Besides, I'll need enough dinero to last me awhile. Think I know where I can get it, too."

"Coghlin?" Maxwell growled. "Goddamn, Billy, him and Dobson ain't to be trusted! You don't want to risk that."

"Who they gonna tell?" The Kid gave him a grotesque smile. One side of his mouth curled upward, while the other side remained fixed and hard. "Don't worry, Pete. When they hear I'm headed south of the border, they'll come through and glad to oblige. Probably wet their drawers with relief."

"They'd a sight rather see you dead, and that ain't no lie."

"Won't happen, Pete. Them fellers know I'd talk a blue streak if they ever crossed me. You'll see! All I got to do is send one of your boys into town and they'll pony up so fast it'll make your head swim."

"You always was too goddamn nervy for your own good, Billy."

The Kid roared laughter. "Well, old man, there ain't nobody punched my ticket yet, have they?"

"Oh, Luke, for heaven's sake!"

Ellen Nesbeth looked at him, her eyes full of dark amusement. They were seated on the porch swing, shadowy figures in the early evening twilight. A cool breeze drifted in from the river, and with it the strains of a guitar. The sound of laughter and voices carried clearly from the bunkhouse quadrangle.

"Honestly, you did your best! What more could anyone ask?"

"That won't cut it," Starbuck muttered. "Not by half."

"Don't be silly." She sighed, then straightened her shoulders. "Sometimes I think you are the most exasperating man I ever met. You've done everything humanly possible. Even Mr. Chisum says so! You heard him yourself."

"Then I reckon humanly possible isn't enough.

Not where the Kid's concerned, anyway."

Starbuck had returned to the Jinglebob late last night. A shave and a hot bath, along with a change of clothes, had restored his outward appearance. But inwardly he was gripped by a deep melancholy. All day he had brooded around the house, withdrawn and miserable, and clearly in no mood to talk. Only after supper, at Ellen's insistence, had he agreed to venture outside. He gave the impression of a man who had looked within and found himself wanting.

"Let me ask you something, Luke. Have you ever failed at anything before? Anything at all in your entire life!"

Starbuck caught her eye for an instant, looked quickly away. "What's that got to do with the price of tea?"

"You haven't, have you?"

"No, by God, I haven't! So what?"

"Well, just look around you sometime. The world is full of men who haven't done anything but fail! If this is your first time, then count your lucky stars. You've been keeping very special company!"

"I don't give three hoots—"

The sound of hoofbeats silenced him, then a horse suddenly loomed out of the night. John Poe sawed at the reins, skidding to a dust-smothered halt, and leaped from the saddle. He ran toward the house.

Starbuck rose and went to meet him. "What's up? I thought we agreed you'd wet-nurse Garrett."

"Luke—" Poe caught his breath, started over.

"Garrett got a tip on the Kid! I made him swear he'd wait till we got back, then I rode like a bat out of hell. Figgered that was the only way we'd keep him from messin' it up the way he done before."

"Slow down." Starbuck stopped him with an upraised palm. "Now, let's begin at the beginning. What kind of tip?"

"A note under the office door. Garrett found it this morning. Wasn't signed, but it's the genuine article."

"What makes you think so?"

"Was you at Fort Sumner early yesterday?"

Starbuck stared at him, astounded. "How did you know that?"

"From the note," Poe said evenly. "Whoever wrote it said that would prove it's on the level. I got no idea who's behind it, but evidently the Kid was there and you showin' up somehow flushed him."

"The Kid—" Starbuck suddenly grinned. "The Kid's at Fort Sumner?"

"What the hell you think I'm tryin' to tell you? Somebody went to a lot of trouble to make us believe it's gospel truth."

"No, John," Starbuck corrected him. "Somebody went to a lot of trouble to get the Kid killed."

"Well, one thing's for damn sure. We got no time to argue about it! Garrett ain't gonna wait forever."

"Have somebody saddle my horse, and get yourself a fresh one while you're about it. I'll be with you directly."

Poe hurried off toward the corral, leading his horse. Starbuck turned and walked back across the porch. Ellen was still sitting in the swing, her hands folded in her lap. She smiled, something merry lurking in her eyes.

"Apparently you only thought you'd failed."

"We'll see," Starbuck remarked. "I haven't got him yet."

"You will." Her voice trembled slightly. "Just look after yourself and don't get . . . careless . . . Come back safe."

"Count on it." Starbuck hesitated, looking directly into her eyes, then nodded. "You're mighty pretty when you cry."

He stepped off the veranda, and a moment later vanished into the night. A tear rolled down her cheek, but she sat perfectly still, listening. She heard, somewhere far in the darkness, the faint chime of his spurs.

CHAPTER 16

Nightfall settled swiftly over Fort Sumner. A dog barked in the distance, and the murmur of voices carried distinctly from the saloon. The rest of the settlement lay quiet and still under an indigo sky.

Across the parade ground, now overgrown with weeds, were several abandoned buildings. One of them, an old and decaying barracks, afforded a perfect vantage point opposite the saloon. Crouched inside the barracks door, Starbuck and Garrett maintained a silent vigil. Neither man spoke, and a strained, almost palpable air of tension hung between them. Their eyes were fixed on the saloon; they watched the shadowy figures visible through the lamp-lit windows. Their wait, prolonged beyond anything they'd expected, seemed unendurable.

Shortly before sundown, accompanied by John Poe, they had halted a mile south of Fort Sumner. There, leaving their horses tied in a grove of trees, they had begun a cautious approach on foot. As dusk fell, and the supper hour slipped past, they stealthily made their way through the settlement. Once inside the barracks, they had mounted watch on the saloon, where Pete Maxwell's vaqueros normally congregated following the evening meal. Their plan, agreed upon earlier, was based on what seemed a reasonable assumption. If the Kid was hiding out at Fort Sumner, he would almost certainly be drawn to the saloon. Never one to drink alone, he preferred the coarse good humor of rough men. And with Maxwell's vaqueros there was no need for vigilance. He was among friends.

For an hour or more, the lawman had quietly observed as vaqueros began gathering in the saloon. Arriving singly and in small groups, none of those who entered the saloon bore any apparent resemblance to the Kid. But as twilight faded and the night sky grew darker, it became increasingly difficult to distinguish one form from another. The vaqueros tended to be short and slight of build, as was the Kid; from across the parade ground, particularly in the poor light, everyone looked very much alike. Finally, when full night descended, Starbuck began wondering if they hadn't somehow missed spotting the Kid. Troubled by the thought, he'd sent Poe to scout the saloon from the outside. Under the circumstances, it had seemed the only sensible course of action.

Yet now, awaiting Poe's return, all he could think of was a smoke. He hadn't had a cigarette since before sundown, and the interminable passage of time had whetted his craving minute by minute. Then too, he'd been in the saddle almost twenty-four hours straight, with little to eat and no rest.

Supper last night at the Jinglebob seemed a lifetime ago; his stomach growled in protest, and hunger merely aggravated his need for a cigarette. He suddenly envied Poe, and wished he had a taste for chewing tobacco. A jaw stuffed with Red Devil seemed a comforting thought. Or at the very least a distraction. He had a hunch they were in for a long night.

A burst of laughter from the saloon caught his attention. Voices were raised in a volley of Spanish, most of which he found unintelligible, and the commotion slowly subsided. Then, seemingly from nowhere, John Poe materialized out of the night and stepped through the doorway.

"Any luck?" Garrett demanded anxiously. "Was he there?"

"Nope," Poe replied. "All Mex, except the barkeep. No sign of the Kid."

"Damn!"

Garrett stumped away, halting by a window, and stood glowering out across the parade ground. Starbuck and Poe exchanged a worried look. All day, like a man nursing a toothache, Garrett had been crabby and on edge. The protracted wait had further frayed his nerves, and they were reminded that he hadn't the temperament necessary for a manhunt. His patience was clearly exhausted, and worse, there was a smell of fear about him. He seemed terrified that the Kid would elude them, and his spooky behavior was definite cause for alarm. A case of the jitters often got the wrong man killed.

With an oath, he turned and walked back to them. He halted, scowling at Starbuck. "I'm done waitin'! We could sit here all night and not know anything more than we do now."

"What do you suggest?"

"I say we go have a talk with Pete Maxwell. If the Kid's here, he could tell us exactly where to look."

"What makes you think Maxwell will talk? He wouldn't give me the time of day when I was here before."

"He'll talk or I'll bust him upside the goddamn head!"

"You figure that'll turn the trick, do you?"

"It might," Garrett said gruffly. "If it don't, then we ain't lost nothin'. We can keep watch from his house just as easy as we can here."

Starbuck studied him a moment. "All right, Pat, we'll give it a try. But you've got to promise me one thing."

"What's that?"

"Stick a pillow in his mouth before you bust him upside the head. Otherwise you're liable to raise just enough racket to scare the Kid off."

Garrett agreed, and Starbuck led the way out of the barracks. Walking single file, they ghosted from building to building, hugging the shadows. There were no lights in Pete Maxwell's home.

* * *

Saval Gutierrez and his wife, Maria, went to bed around nine. A man of rigid habits, Gutierrez always retired early, for his workday began at the first light of dawn. He was Maxwell's *caporal*, responsible for the entire cattle operation, and he allowed nothing to interfere with his normal routine. That included his friend and houseguest, *El Chivato*.

Bonney was seated at the kitchen table. The lamp-wick was turned low and he idly stirred a cup of coffee, now grown cold. His lopsided features were glum and his expression was vaguely abstracted. He stared at a fly crawling across the rough-hewn wooden table.

Nearly two days had passed since he'd sent the message to Joe Coghlin. The reply, brought back by the vaquero who had ridden into Lincoln, was affirmative and seemingly reasonable. Coghlin promised a large sum—at least $5,000—but pleaded a momentary shortage of cash. He asked for time, no more than a day or so, and gave every assurance that the money would be forthcoming. He indicated that Earl Gantry would personally make the delivery, using Maxwell as a go-between. All within a couple of days.

At first heartened, Bonney had congratulated himself on his assessment of Coghlin and Dobson. Much as he'd suspected, they were willing to pay quite handsomely to see the last of him. Moreover, with $5,000 in his kick, he could live high on the hog in Mexico. In a land where a thousand pesos was considered a fortune, he would be filthy rich, without a care in the world. His mind turned to visions of sloe-eyed señoritas and long nights of revelry, and an end to running from the law.

Except for Starbuck, he might have stayed on at Fort Sumner indefinitely. The game of cat-and-mouse he'd played with Garrett was almost laughable, little more than a diversion. There was an ironic twist about it that also appealed to his warped humor. For the past two months he had been an honored guest in the home of Pat Garrett's brother-in-law. Saval Gutierrez, who was married to the older sister of Garrett's wife, detested the lawman. Like everyone else at the settlement, he believed Garrett had sold out to the *gringo politicos*, and he took pride in harboring the territory's most wanted outlaw. A simple man, Gutierrez considered it both an act of defiance and a grand joke. One day he planned to tell his upstart brother-in-law that it was he who had provided sanctuary for *El Chivato*.

Yet now, seated alone in the kitchen, Bonney no longer found it a jesting matter. Since late afternoon, he'd begun to have second thoughts about Coghlin. It seemed to him suspicious that the money hadn't been delivered; he could think of no reason for Coghlin to stall, unless the purpose was to hold him at Fort Sumner. That went against his judgment of Coghlin—who had a great deal to lose by betraying him—but he could hardly afford to discount the possibility. He had survived by trusting no one who might profit from his death. And tonight, all his instincts told him the time had come and gone for trusting Joe Coghlin.

Pondering on it, a sudden image of Starbuck fleeted through his mind. He feared no man; but he respected Starbuck's dogged determination to kill him; and the odds of that happening had increased greatly over the last three days. The money Coghlin had promised abruptly ceased to be a factor in the scheme of things. He would borrow whatever he could from Maxwell, and put Fort Sumner behind him long before dawn. A few days in the saddle, careful to watch his backtrail, and then . . .

Adios and goodbye. Hello, Mexico!

Bonney grinned, satisfied he'd made the right decision. And having made it, he saw no reason to delay a moment longer. He stood, moving to the back door, and stepped outside. He walked toward Pete Maxwell's house.

On the porch, Starbuck and Poe stood gazing at the distant lights of the saloon. Neither of them had spoken since Garrett entered the house. Only a few minutes had elapsed, but they assumed Maxwell was undergoing some rough and heavy-handed form of interrogation. Given Garrett's mood, it seemed the most likely prospect.

A figure suddenly rounded the corner of the house and stepped onto the porch. They turned, startled by the sound, but he saw them an instant before they could collect themselves. His hand moved, and they heard the metallic whirr of a Colt hammer thumbed to full-cock. He stared at them, unable to distinguish their features in the pitch dark.

"*¿Quién es?*"

Starbuck thought he recognized the voice, but he hesitated. Spanish somehow changed the inflection, and he wasn't certain enough to risk killing one of Maxwell's vaqueros. Nor was he anxious to get himself killed. The shadowy figure had the drop on them, and he willed Poe not to make any sudden moves.

"*¿Quién es?*"

The tone was harsher now, more demanding. Starbuck squinted hard, trying desperately to identify the face behind the voice. Only a blurred shape was visible, however, and he forced himself to remain quiet. Poe once more followed his lead.

With the gun trained on them, the figure moved sideways across the porch. No one spoke, and as in some strange ritual dance, the lawmen froze still as statues while the figure scuttled crablike past them. Then, before they realized his intent, the door opened and closed. He was inside the house.

The voice was distinct and unmistakable to the men in the bedroom. Pete Maxwell lay immobile, propped up against his pillow and scared witless. The snout of a pistol barrel was pressed firmly to his temple, and the hand behind it was shaking. Garrett, round-eyed and scarcely daring to breathe, sat in a wooden chair beside the bed. He watched as the figure sidled through the door and stopped. The voice he knew better than his own spoke.

"¿Quienes son esos hombres afuera, Pete?"

Garrett swung the pistol around. His hand was trembling violently, and he felt a warm trickle running down his leg. He fired, hurling himself sideways out of the chair. He struck the floor, frantically thumbing the hammer back, and triggered a second shot. A streak of flame exploded from the muzzle, and in the flash of light he saw a figure slumping forward, knees buckled. An instant later he heard the soft thud of a body hitting the floor.

Starbuck and Poe had entered the house at the sound of gunfire. Flattened against the wall outside the bedroom, they waited in a void of eerie black silence. At last, hearing nothing, Starbuck edged closer to the door.

"Pat! You all right?"

A muffled voice answered. "I think the Kid's down."

"Maxwell!" Starbuck rapped out. "Can you hear me?"

"Yeah," Maxwell replied softly. "I hear you."

"Light a lamp! Pronto!"

A long moment passed. Then a match flared in the darkness. The cider glow of a lamp slowly lighted the bedroom. Starbuck took a quick look, scanning the room in one swift glance. Maxwell cowered against the headboard, the burnt match still clutched in his hand. Hugging the floor, Garrett lay prone beside the bed. His eyes were wild and his pistol was pointed across the room. A still form was sprawled face down near the opposite wall.

Starbuck entered the room. He kept his pistol trained on the fallen man, approaching step by step while Poe covered him from the door. He scooped a Colt Lightning off the floor, then hooked a toe under the dead man's arm and rolled him onto his back. A bright red splotch was centered on the Kid's chest. His eyes were open, sightless.

"Is he dead?"

Garrett climbed to his feet, took a shaky step forward. Starbuck turned, watching him, then nodded. "He won't get any deader, Pat."

"Jesus." Garrett righted the overturned chair, and sat down heavily. "I knew it was him the minute I heard his voice. Then he busted in here and I figured my time had come sure as hell."

"Was that when he fired?"

"No." Garrett looked puzzled. "What're you talkin' about? The Kid never got off a shot."

Starbuck holstered his own gun and smelled the muzzle of the Colt Lightning. "You're right." He glanced up, one eye cocked in a sardonic squint. "It hasn't been fired. Guess he never knew what hit him."

"So what?" Garrett muttered, slightly shame-faced. "He wouldn't have give me no better chance. I had to get him before he got me!"

"Don't get touchy, Pat. In your place, I suppose I would've done it exactly the same way."

"Bet your sweet ass you would! One peep out of me and he'd have let go without blinkin' an eye."

Starbuck looked at the body without expression. He reflected a moment, then turned and handed Garrett the unfired gun. "Well, Pat, I reckon the Kid's worries are over. Wish to hell I could say the same for us."

"What's that supposed to mean?"

Starbuck stared past him at Maxwell. "Billy contacted someone in Lincoln, didn't he?" When Maxwell nodded, he went on in a cold voice. "Whoever it was informed on him slipped a note under the sheriff's door. That's what brought us here and that's what got him killed. You care to give me a name?"

"Joe Coghlin," Maxwell said vindictively. "Billy was set to hightail it for Mexico. He asked Coghlin for money, and Coghlin promised to send it along by Earl Gantry. Looks like he sent you instead."

"It figures." He glanced quickly at Garrett. "There's your answer, Pat. They got the Kid and now they'll try for the Nesbeths. A clean sweep."

"How you aim to stop 'em?"

A ghost of a smile touched Starbuck's mouth. "The same way you stopped the Kid. Only a little different."

CHAPTER 17

Everyone gathered in the parlor. Their manner was somber, and they sat down as if assembling for a last supper. Starbuck had expected a lighter mood, but apparently the Kid's death struck them as a bad omen. He walked to the fireplace and began rolling a smoke.

Chisum took a rocker, his pipe clamped between his teeth like a bone. Fred and Erma Nesbeth huddled together on the settee, their eyes darting nervously around the room. The two girls looked daggers at each other. Sallie was stiffly proper, her ankles crossed beneath her skirt and her hands folded demurely in her lap. Ellen, by contrast, appeared ready for battle, with the icy stare of a vixen defending her den. An oppressive air of uncertainty and tension hung over the group, like strangers brought together to witness a beheading.

Starbuck twisted the ends on the cigarette and stuck it in his mouth. With Poe, he had ridden straight through from Fort Sumner, and he was still covered with a grimy layer of trail dust. Last night, listening to the women of the settlement mourn *El*

Chivato's death, he had slept badly. And tonight, watching the Nesbeths fidget on the settee, he was filled with a sense of misgiving. He wondered if any man had the right to toy with other people's lives, and the thought itself, alien to his very character, further compounded his apprehension. So long as his own purpose was served, he had never before considered the hardship it might impose on others. He found this new concern troublesome, almost impossible to believe of himself. He saw it as a weakness, and yet he was not a weak man. The sensation gave him a moment's pause.

At length, with no real idea how it would end, he lit his cigarette and began talking. He briefly related the events leading to those last moments in Pete Maxwell's bedroom. He told them how the Kid had died, and noted that Garrett had given permission for the young outlaw to be buried at Fort Sumner. Then, stressing the words, he repeated Maxwell's statement regarding Joe Coghlin. There was no doubt whatever that Coghlin and Dobson, in league with Judge Owen Hough, had arranged the Kid's death.

"Of course," he concluded, "the only new evidence we've got is the vaquero that delivered the message to Coghlin. Anything the Kid said to Maxwell would be ruled hearsay. So it's not much, maybe nothing."

"Nothing!" Chisum rumbled. "Why, it's—uh—cor—cor—aww hell, Sallie, what's the word I'm searchin' for?"

"Corroboration," Sallie said brightly. "Testimony that tends to substantiate previous testimony."

"Damn right!" Chisum affirmed. "That vaquero can back up everything the Nesbeths testify to. We've got a link between Coghlin and the Kid, and we've got it in spades!"

"I don't know," Starbuck said doubtfully. "Granted, it'll help, but it's still pretty circumstantial. Coghlin will deny it, so it'll boil down to a matter of their word against his."

"Judas Priest!" Chisum yelled. "You should've thought of that before you and Garrett killed our best witness."

"The Kid called the tune," Starbuck observed. "Besides, his lips were sewed shut long before that, and we all know it."

There was a time of stony silence. Chisum puffed on his pipe, eyes slitted against the smoke. He was clearly disgruntled, but Starbuck held his gaze, waiting him out. After a long while Chisum gestured with his pipe, as though dismissing a matter of no consequence. His eyes softened and his features assumed a visage aged by tolerance. His gaze shuttled around the room, then settled on the Nesbeths. He smiled, and regarded them with a look of benign wisdom.

"Luke and me seem to be at loggerheads, but don't you folks let that fool you. We both want them fellers in Lincoln. Want 'em so bad it makes our teeth hurt! Course mine are store bought, so that kind of gives Luke the worst of it."

Everyone smiled dutifully at the joke. He chuckled, eyes still fixed on the settee, then resumed. "Now, Fred, Mrs. Nesbeth"—he suddenly remembered the girl—"you too, Ellen! Here's the way I see things. The Kid would've strengthened our case, but we're still in good shape without him. Your testimony—added to the rustled cows we found and the testimony of Maxwell's vaquero—all of that wouldn't leave a jury no choice but to bring in a guilty verdict. Course, we got an ace in the hole I ain't even mentioned yet."

He gave the Nesbeths a slow, conspiratorial nod. "You've heard the sayin' about rats deserting a sinking ship. Well, that's exactly what'll happen! Once we jail them fellers—Coghlin and Dobson, especially Gantry!—one of 'em will start talkin'. Pretty soon they'll all be out to save their own skins, and we'll have 'em beggin' us to make a deal. See, contrary to what you've always heard, there really ain't no honor among thieves. You folks can take my word on it."

Fred and Erma Nesbeth shifted uncomfortably on the settee. They were aware Chisum was awaiting a response, but they avoided his gaze. Finally, Fred Nesbeth coughed, clearing his throat, and looked at Starbuck.

"Luke, you've always treated us square, and I'd like to hear what you got to say. Do you go along with Mr. Chisum?"

Starbuck was torn between conscience and expediency. He took a long pull on his cigarette, exhaled slowly. "A couple of days ago I figured to get the Kid and call it quits. But now that he's dead, it turns out that wasn't enough. I want the men behind him—for personal reasons—so I'm not sure I could give you a straight answer."

"You just did," Nesbeth said evenly. "We knowed all along you had a personal score to settle, but we trust you, Luke. So go on and tell us how it looks to you. That's all we're askin'."

"Well, first off," Starbuck said in a deliberate voice, "there're no guarantees. You've got to understand your lives will be in danger from start to finish. There's nothing they won't do to keep you from testifying."

"I reckon we done figured that out, Luke."

"All right." Starbuck paused, choosing his words. "The next thing you ought to consider is whether or not we'll get a conviction. I'd say the odds are fifty-fifty, strictly a toss-up. Everything we've got is circumstantial, no hard evidence." He flipped his hand back and forth. "A jury might buy it, and then again, they might not. We wouldn't know till they brought in a verdict. It'd be just that close."

"Go on," Nesbeth prompted. "We're still listenin'."

Starbuck flicked an ash off his cigarette, thoughtful. "I'd have to say you can't count on that bunch turning against one another. Coghlin's the weak link, but we would have to run a mighty good bluff before he'd crack. All depends on the breaks and how we handle it. Like I said, no guarantees."

"No guarantees," Nesbeth repeated hollowly. "Anything else?"

"One more thing. Whether you go ahead or pull out, I'll stick by you right down the line. Anybody gets to you, they'll have to get past me first. That's the one thing I'll give you my word on."

Ellen Nesbeth looked startled. In all the time she'd known him, she had never once suspected that Starbuck could feel compassion for anyone. His emotions were buried so deep—sealed off by a hard stoicism—that he appeared immune to all forms of sentiment. Yet now, to her profound shock, he had actually taken pity on her parents. By telling the truth, he risked dissuading them from the very thing he wanted. And still, he had offered them a way out. She marveled at the change, and wondered if perhaps she hadn't misjudged him all along. She felt a sudden outpouring of affection. Her heartbeat quickened and she sensed there was no turning away.

"Listen to him, Daddy." She looked directly at her father. "Luke won't let us down. He never has and he never will."

"Ellen's right," Erma Nesbeth said firmly. "We've trusted him this far, and there's no call to back out now. You do like she says, Fred."

Nesbeth grinned weakly and threw up his hands. "Well, Luke, what's a feller to do? You got my womenfolk convinced, and I reckon that's good enough for me. We'll play along till you tell us different."

"You're sure?" Starbuck pressed him. "I wouldn't want to think I'd talked you into it."

"We're sure," Nesbeth said, glancing at his wife and daughter. "Learned a long time ago not to go against female intuition. Gets a man in a passel of trouble every time he tries it."

"Well now!" Chisum beamed, giving them a nut-cracker grin. "That's dandy, just dandy. We'll teach them fellers in Lincoln a thing or two they won't never forget!"

Starbuck took a last drag on his cigarette and tossed it into the fireplace. He felt Ellen's gaze on him, but he avoided her eyes. His misgiving, suddenly stronger than before, gave him an uncomfortable moment. He wasn't at all certain he'd done the right thing.

A short while later he met with Poe and Chisum in the cattleman's study. Chisum was in high spirits, his features ruddy with excitement. Seated in his usual chair, he appraised Starbuck with a shrewd glance.

"That was pretty slick the way you let them talk themselves into it. Yessir, Luke—pretty damn slick!"

"Let's get something straight." There was a hard edge to Starbuck's tone. "If the Nesbeths had backed out, I was ready to get them the hell and gone from here right now. And if things start going wrong, I aim to do just that."

"What the hell are you talkin' about?"

"I'm saying it better go smooth as silk. Otherwise I'll get them out of the territory so fast you won't have time to pucker up and whistle."

"Bullfeathers!" Chisum admonished him. "There ain't nothin' gonna happen, Luke. With you and the boys guardin' them, nobody would have the nerve to try!"

"Well, I guess we'll just have to wait and see, won't we?"

Starbuck didn't relish the thought of taking the Nesbeths into Lincoln. The idea was studded with danger, and he knew their lives would be in jeopardy the entire time. But there was no way around it, no alternative. To bring criminal charges, the Nesbeths had to appear in court. The only choice was when, and under what circumstances. Which gave him a chance, however slim, to stack the deck in their favor.

He turned to Poe. "I want you to ride into town tonight. Tell Garrett to arrest Coghlin and Gantry tomorrow. You bird-dog him, and make sure he gets them locked up by sundown."

Poe appeared skeptical. "What's the rush?"

"Surprise," Starbuck said bluntly. "With the Kid dead, they won't expect us to move so fast. I want them jailed no later than dark tomorrow night. Understand?"

"Whatever you say, Luke."

"Don't let me down. I plan on slipping the Nesbeths into town sometime after dark. We'll put them up at the hotel and keep them surrounded with guards."

He reflected a moment, massaging his jaw. When he spoke, his voice was low and urgent. "John, it's got to come off like clockwork. One mistake and the Nesbeths will wind up in a funeral parlor. So tell Garrett to arrange a court appearance for early the next morning. I want that preliminary hearing over and done with before anyone's the wiser."

"Sounds good to me," Poe acknowledged. "What happens after the hearing?"

"We separate Coghlin and Gantry, and start working on them one at a time. By then, they'll have a fair case of the jitters, and we ought to be able to run a decent bluff. Assuming one of them breaks, we'll arrest Dobson and Hough on conspiracy charges. Then we'll start offering deals and see who talks the loudest."

Starbuck took a moment to repeat his instructions, stressing the need for speed and secrecy. Poe left the room immediately afterwards, and went to prepare for the ride into Lincoln. When he was gone, Chisum fired up his pipe, puffing thoughtfully. He regarded Starbuck with a speculative look.

"I didn't hear nothin' about what happens if Coghlin don't break. You got any ideas on that score?"

Starbuck's eyes narrowed. "If he won't talk, then I reckon we'll stop playing rough and start playing dirty."

"I ain't sure I follow you."

"Why, it's simple enough. I'll forget the rules and do it my own way."

"Quit talkin' riddles! What way is that?"

"Judge Colt and the jury of six. Verdict guaranteed."

She was waiting for him by the river. Her legs were drawn up and her chin rested on her knees. He sat down, saying nothing, and for a long while they stared out across the water. Presently, with a contented sigh, she turned her head and looked at him. Her eyes appeared misty in the dim starlight.

"You had me fooled until tonight."

"How so?"

"I thought you didn't have a drop of mercy in you. But I was wrong. Underneath that tough act, you're really a softy, aren't you?"

He smiled. "What makes you say that?"

"You gave my folks a chance to change their minds. That wasn't the Luke Starbuck I thought I knew."

"What makes you think tonight wasn't an act?"

"I don't understand."

"Well, the way it works out, I'll be taking you and your folks into Lincoln tomorrow. Maybe I rigged things tonight just to keep everybody on the string. That'd mean I fooled you into thinking you'd been fooled. Wouldn't it?"

She laughed happily. "You aren't fooling me

now, either! But don't worry, I won't tell anyone. Your secret's safe with me."

"Cross your heart?"

She crossed her heart. Then she lay back on the grassy river bank, her eyes laving him with a look of tenderness. When she spoke, her voice was almost inaudible, entreating him with a shy, virginal innocence.

"Luke, make love to me; let me love you."

He took her in his arms and embraced her. She helped him with the buttons and stays, and he slowly undressed her. When she lay naked before him, he dropped his gunbelt on the ground and quickly removed his clothes. Then he stretched out beside her, gathering her once more in his arms.

Her mouth opened and she pulled his head down. Their tongues met and dueled, then he took one of her breasts in his mouth and sucked the nipple erect. Her hand grasped his manhood, now hard and gorged with blood, and she stroked it with a gentle caressing motion. He probed the moist bog between her legs, teasing the cleft where it parted within an abundant swell of flesh. She exhaled a hoarse gasp and they came together in an agonized clash of loins. Her legs spidered around him and he slipped into her, found his motion. His strokes quickened and he thrust deeper and she jolted upward to meet him. Her hips moved faster and faster, lunging and insistent, until at last she could hold back no longer. She clutched his flanks, ramming him to the very core of herself, and together they exploded in a mol-

ten rush, blinded and feverishly holding tighter in
that last instant. Forever passed, then he rolled away
one arm around her waist, her head pillowed on his
shoulder. She shuddered and he hugged her and
they lay entwined, silently joined by the warmth of
a quenched flame.

He thought no thoughts of tomorrow.

CHAPTER 18

Starbuck led the way into town. The Nesbeths, seated in a buckboard, trailed him by several yards. His men flanked the buckboard, two at the front and two at the rear. They were positioned to shield the Nesbeths, and their eyes were constantly on the move.

Only moments before, the last rays of dusk had been leeched from the sky. Nightfall lay over Lincoln, and the town's few streetlamps were now lighted. The stores were closed, and aside from the saloons, the business district was quiet. Several passersby, hurrying home to supper, glanced at the strange caravan as it proceeded uptown. The only sound was the muffled thud of hoofbeats on the dusty street.

At the hotel, Ellen and Mrs. Nesbeth were assisted from the buckboard. Then, with the guards formed in a tight phalanx, they trooped into the lobby. Starbuck motioned them to wait by the stairs and walked toward the front desk. Through a doorway on the opposite side of the lobby, he noted the dining room was doing a lively supper trade. Halting at the desk, he nodded to the night clerk.

"I'd like four rooms on the second floor."

"Yes, sir, Mr. Starbuck." The clerk darted a glance at the Nesbeths. "Any special room order . . . for the ladies?"

"No," Starbuck said without elaboration. "But the rooms have to be off the street side of the hotel, and I want them all in a row, next door to each other."

The clerk took a minute to produce the keys. He laid them on the desk. "There you are, Mr. Starbuck. Upstairs and down the hall on the left."

"Is there a back entrance on the second floor?"

"Upstairs—?" The clerk gave him an odd look. "No, sir, not upstairs. The only other entrance is the back door to the kitchen."

Starbuck spun the room ledger and scrawled his name. "We'll stay the night, maybe longer. Anybody asks, you just tell them the rooms are in my name."

He turned and crossed the lobby. Handing the keys to Frank Miller, he pointed to the staircase. "Hike upstairs and check out these rooms. While you're there, make sure there's no way to get into the building from the rear."

Without waiting for a reply, he jerked his chin at Jessie Tuttle and moved off to one side. "Here's the way we'll work it, Jessie. Take the Nesbeths to supper"—he indicated the dining room—"then get them upstairs and locked in their rooms. I want two guards in the hall at all times, no more than four-hour shifts. Put the Nesbeths in the center rooms, and you boys split up in the rooms on either side of them. One man sleeps while his partner stands watch, one on and one off, all night. Got it?"

Tuttle bobbed his head. "You ain't stickin' around for supper?"

"I'll eat after I get things squared away over at the jail. Might take a while, so you boys keep your eyes open and brace anybody that comes near those rooms. Act polite, but don't take any chances. Unless they're registered in the hotel, they've got no business up there."

Ellen Nesbeth approached, halting beside them. Starbuck nodded to Tuttle, who quickly rejoined the others near the stairway. She waited until he was out of earshot before she spoke.

"Are you expecting trouble?"

"No," Starbuck assured her. "Not tonight anyway. With Coghlin and Gantry in jail, it'll take Judge Hough a while to get things sorted out."

"Then why so serious?"

"Well, it impresses the boys, keeps them on their toes. I've got to have a talk with Garrett, and I'm liable to be gone—"

"Not too late, I hope?"

"All depends." Starbuck caught something in her voice. "What makes you ask?"

"You did get me a separate room, didn't you?"

"Yeah—"

"Good!" A slow smile warmed her face. "Then you can come tuck me in when you get back."

"How do you suggest I get past the boys? They'll be standing guard outside your door."

"You'll think of something!" Her eyes suddenly shone, and she laughed. "After last night, I'll be very insulted if you don't!"

Starbuck had given a good deal of thought to last night. Their lovemaking had touched him in a way that left him unsettled, vaguely disturbed. Never before had he considered the possibility that one woman might satisfy him in all things. He was a loner by nature, and he'd always assumed he would live out his life footloose and unencumbered. Yet, there on the riverbank last night, he had realized there was something more between them than physical attraction. She was an unusually spirited woman, with the gamy wit and resolute manner to match his own. And like him, she cared nothing for convention or the social restraints others imposed on themselves. In that, as well as their general outlook on life, they were very much birds of a feather. He wasn't certain where it would lead them, nor was he entirely comfortable with wanting someone, the sensation of need. He only knew he wanted time, with her and with himself. Time to determine who she was. And what she meant to him.

"You're right," he said at length, grinning. "I'll think of something. One way or another—"

"Any way at all!" she interrupted, her voice low and vibrant. "I'll be waiting . . . all night."

Frank Miller appeared on the stairs. As he approached them, Ellen gave Starbuck a secretive wink and rejoined her parents. Miller's report required only a moment: he had inspected the upper floor thoroughly and found everything in order. Satisfied, Starbuck placed Tuttle in charge, and waited while the Nesbeths were escorted into the dining room. Then he turned and walked from the hotel.

Outside, he hurried toward the courthouse. As he moved along the boardwalk, his thoughts centered on Coghlin and Gantry. He briefly considered trying to bluff them into a confession on their first night in jail. But then, curbing his impatience, he decided to hold to to the original plan. Tomorrow, once they were formally charged, would be the time to offer them a deal. He crossed the street and moved along the walkway to the courthouse steps.

The door to the sheriff's office was open. The instant he entered the room, he sensed something had gone wrong. Poe was slouched down in a rickety armchair, and Garrett was seated behind the desk. Neither of them spoke, but they exchanged a quick hangdog look. His gaze settled on John Poe.

"All right, let's have it! What's the problem?"

"Earl Gantry," Poe said, painfully embarrassed. We arrested Coghlin this morning, but there's no sign of Gantry. The sonovabitch pulled a vanishing act."

"Tell me about it."

"Nothin' much to tell. By the time we got out to Coghlin's ranch, Gantry was long gone. We searched the place from one end to the other, but it didn't do no good. All the hands just dummied up and gave us the silent routine."

"Keep talking," Starbuck said sternly. "There's more to it than that."

"Don't blame him," Garrett interjected. "Word gets around damn quick, Luke. By the time we arrested Coghlin and got him locked up, the news was all over town."

"You're saying Gantry got wind of it somehow?"

"Hell, he must've!" Garrett blustered. "More'n likely Dobson sent a rider to warn him. We weren't exactly loafin' around, but all he needed was a few minutes' head start."

"Well, Pat," Starbuck said woodenly, "from what you say, he had time to spare and then—"

The dull roar of a shotgun sounded somewhere in the distance. A second blast followed almost instantaneously, then silence. Starbuck whirled toward the door, ordering Garrett to watch the jail. With Poe at his heels, he ran from the courthouse and turned uptown.

A few moments later they pounded into the hotel lobby. The door to the dining room was blocked with people, their faces stamped with a look of ghoulish absorption. From inside, someone moaned and another voice ripped out a savage curse. One of the onlookers suddenly backed away, gagging violently, and retched his supper on the lobby floor.

Starbuck shouldered a path through the crowd. In the doorway he slammed to an abrupt halt, momentarily undone by the grisly scene before him. His features colored, one moment ashen and the next dark with rage. His vision glazed and blood roared in his ears as he stared at the carnage.

Fred and Erma Nesbeth had been blown out of their chairs. They lay sprawled on the floor, their clothes splotched with dark stains. Ellen sat perfectly still, her eyes rolled back in her head and her arms dangling loosely at her sides. The front of her dress was pocked with small dots the color of wine. Frank Miller, seated beside her, was slumped across the table. A single ball had punched through his skull, splattering bone and brain matter over the checkered tablecloth. Another of the guards was down, blood pumping from his neck, and Tuttle had a napkin pressed to the wound. The last man, untouched, stood watching in a hollow-eyed daze.

Starbuck finally collected himself. He crossed the room, followed closely by Poe, careful to keep his gaze averted from the girl. They halted near the table as Jessie Tuttle rose and flung the bloody napkin aside. He looked at them, tears streaming down his face.

"Couldn't stop the bleeding. He's gone, Luke. Dead."

For a moment no one spoke. They stood in a tight circle, unable to look at each other or the gruesome shambles around them. Then, his voice calm but insistent, Starbuck grasped Tuttle's arm.

"Tell me what happened, Jessie. All of it, start to finish."

"We were havin' supper—" Tuttle's voice cracked and he swallowed hard.

"Go on, you were having supper. What happened next?"

Tuttle told it quickly, the details fragmented yet agonizingly clear. The Nesbeths and their guards were seated at a table near the front of the room. A window beside their table—which looked out on a passageway between the hotel and an adjoining building—suddenly blew apart. The first shotgun blast killed Nesbeth and his wife instantly. The second shot, meant for the girl, went wide and claimed two of the guards as well. There was no chance for Tuttle or the remaining guard to return fire. The window exploded in a hail of buckshot, and within the space of a heartbeat, five people lay dead or dying. The killer had done his work and gone before anyone realized he was there.

Starbuck asked several questions, waiting until he was certain Tuttle had control of himself. Then, anxious to have a look at the outside passageway, he left Tuttle and the other guard with the chore of summoning an undertaker. He walked from the hotel, accompanied by Poe, and proceeded directly to the side of the building. There, squatting down, he struck a match and searched the flintlike soil for footprints. Finding nothing, he rose and stood for a time staring through the shattered window. At length, his face a stony mask, he turned to Poe.

"How—?" He choked on his rage, slowly gathered himself, then tried again. "How did they know? No one was told about the Nesbeths."

"Not exactly." Poe looked wretched. "But I got an idea who might've guessed."

"Guessed?" Starbuck's eyes bored into him. "What the hell are you talking about?"

"Hough," Poe said hoarsely. "The circuit judge was called over to White Oaks late yesterday. If he ain't in town, then Hough handles all preliminary hearings. When Garrett told me about it—"

Starbuck spoke through clenched teeth. "You let him ask Hough to schedule a hearing?"

"I didn't see no harm," Poe explained sheepishly. "Coghlin was locked up, and you were already on your way into town. I figgered we'd surprise Hough and show up at the hearing with the Nesbeths. I never thought he'd put two and two together—"

"You should've, John." A vein in Starbuck's temple stood out like twisted cord. "You're too old a hand to underestimate the other fellow."

Poe nodded, his expression downcast. "The minute I saw 'em"—he made a lame gesture in the direction of the window—"the Nesbeths and the boys. Goddamn, Luke. I'd give anything if it'd been me instead of them! I just never figgered—"

He faltered, the words trailing away. Silence thickened between them, and for a moment the breach seemed irreparable. Then Starbuck stepped past him, walking toward the courthouse.

"Let's leave it there, John. We've got work to do."

*   *   *

Garrett looked up as they entered the office. Star-buck halted before the desk and slowly unpinned the badge from his shirt. He stared at it while Garrett and Poe in turn stared at him.

"Pat, I reckon I won't need this now."

"You mean . . . the Nesbeths . . . they got the Nesbeths?"

"Yeah." Starbuck tossed the badge. Garrett caught it, and in the same motion, Starbuck pulled his gun. "Stand up, Pat. Slow and easy, no sudden moves."

"Luke, you've gone off your—"

"Around here!" Starbuck commanded, wagging the gun barrel. "Keep your hands high and move around here. Now!"

Garrett obeyed. He stood, hands over his head, and walked around the desk. Starbuck stepped behind him and eased his pistol from the holster. Then, the snout of his own gun in the lawman's back, he nudged Garrett forward.

"Upstairs, Pat. No funny business or you're liable to spring a leak."

With Poe bringing up the rear, they left the office and mounted the stairs. On the second floor they proceeded to the jail room, pausing to collect the keys off a wall peg. Following Starbuck's instructions, Garrett then unlocked the cell and swung the door open. Joe Coghlin, watching them in stark terror, backed to the far side of the lockup.

"Inside!" Starbuck pushed the lawman through the door. His gaze quickly shifted to Coghlin. "All right, fat man, let's go."

"No, don't." Coghlin cringed against the bars. "I haven't done—"

"Outside!" Starbuck said furiously. "Move it!"

Coghlin warily crossed the cell and stepped through the door. Starbuck halted him there and dropped Garrett's pistol at his feet. Slowly, one click at a time, he thumbed the hammer on his Colt.

"You've got a choice, Coghlin. You can talk or you can be shot while trying to escape. What'll it be?"

"It won't wash!" Coghlin whined. "Nobody would believe that in a hundred years."

"Maybe, maybe not." Starbuck's tone was icy. "Unless you unbutton your lip, you won't be around to find out, will you?"

Coghlin blinked several times. He saw something pitiless and feral in Starbuck's eyes, and knew he was very close to death. He chose life. "I'll talk! Honest to God, the whole story. Everything!"

"One thing." Starbuck's mouth hardened. "One straight answer or you're a dead man. Who ordered the Nesbeths killed?"

"Hough!" Coghlin blurted. "He's the one that called the shots all along. Me and Dobson never had no sayso in nothin'. We just took orders! I swear—"

"Back in the cell."

Coghlin gave him a dumbfounded, doglike stare. "What?"

"I said back in the cell. Get the lead out!"

Coghlin backpedaled through the door. He moved quickly to the bunk and sat down. Starbuck lowered the hammer on his Colt, holstering it, then nodded to Poe. He turned and strode off toward the hall.

"C'mon, Pat! Lock him up, and don't forget your gun."

CHAPTER 19

John Poe recognized all the signs. The quiet manner and the impassive stare. The blunt, menacing cadence of speech, almost as though words were a barrier to be surmounted quickly. The deadly calm and iron determination of a man prepared to kill.

He was frankly amazed that Starbuck hadn't killed Coghlin. He had expected it, and he still had no ready explanation as to why the fat man had been spared. Over the years he had seen men grovel and beg, pleading for their lives, all to no avail. When it had gone that far, there was, to his recollection, no instance of mercy shown. But while Coghlin had escaped with his life, Poe knew he'd read the signs correctly. The Nesbeths' brutal slaying had triggered remorseless anger, and a quiet rage to kill. He could only surmise that Starbuck was after bigger game.

Starbuck stood by the window, rolling a smoke. He struck a match, lighting the cigarette, as the clump of footsteps sounded on the hallway stairs. Garrett stormed into the office, outrage twisting his features into a grimace. He stopped, his voice hectoring and curiously shrill.

"You've got your goddamn nerve! You hear me, Starbuck? You're the sorriest bastard I ever run across, and I've seen 'em all!"

Starbuck stared out the window a moment longer. When he turned, his face was pale and his eyes were grim. "I'm sorry, Pat. I had to make it look convincing, and I wasn't sure you'd go along with me."

"Why the hell didn't you ask? You got no call to humiliate me that way! And I won't stand for it no more! You hear me, Luke? No more!"

"I hear you." Starbuck exhaled smoke, watching him. "You've had your apology, so don't push it."

"Well, that's better!" Garrett muttered, suddenly leery of pressing the matter. "Just so we understand one another. Now, suppose you tell me what you've got up your sleeve. And after that fool stunt, it better be damn good."

"Coghlin just put a rope around Hough's neck. That's good enough for me."

"Aww for Chrissakes! You had a gun on him! You really expect him to come into court and spill his guts the same way?"

"He'll talk," Starbuck said without inflection. "Because if he doesn't, he knows I'll kill him."

Garrett looked surprised. "You weren't jokin', then?"

"No, Pat, I'm fresh out of jokes."

"Awright, let's assume he'll talk. What's next?"

"We need to arrest Dobson and Hough. I'd suggest we split up and do it quick. That way we'll have them both in jail before either one has a chance to run."

"Yeah, that sounds reasonable. Which one you want?"

Starbuck took a long pull on his cigarette. He glanced at Poe, shook his head in an almost imperceptible motion. Then, with a deadpan expression, he looked at Garrett.

"Why don't you take Dobson? I'd sort of like to bring in the judge myself."

"What about Gantry?"

"There's time," Starbuck observed. "Let's get the big dogs and worry about him later."

"Suits me," Garrett said easily. "Ought to be official, though. Suppose you pin that badge back on and we'll forget you ever took it off."

Starbuck hesitated only a moment. Then he crossed the room, took the badge off the desk, and pinned it on his shirt. When he looked around, there was a faint smile at the corners of his mouth.

"Thanks for reminding me, Pat. Wouldn't want it to be unofficial."

"What the hell, Luke, it's all in the line of duty, ain't it? No thanks needed."

Garrett grinned and led the way out of the courthouse. On the street, Starbuck and Poe turned in the direction of the residential district. Garrett, hitching up his gunbelt, walked toward the center of town.

* * *

North of the business district, Starbuck and Poe stopped before a large two-story frame house. The upper floor was dark, but the windows on one side of the ground floor blazed with lamplight. After studying the layout a moment, Starbuck sent Poe to cover the rear of the house. Then he walked to the front door and yanked the pull bell.

From somewhere within the house he heard footsteps. A few seconds elapsed, with the measured tread growing louder, then the door opened. Owen Hough stood framed against a backdrop of light.

"Evening, Judge."

"Deputy." Hough nodded amiably. "Something I can do for you?"

"Garrett thought you might be able to help us out. Have you got a minute?"

"Of course." Hough stepped aside. "Always glad to assist in any way I can."

Starbuck entered, removing his hat. A central hall ran the length of the house. On the left was a staircase to the upper floor, and on the right a door opened onto the parlor. Farther down the hall, a shaft of light spilled through another doorway. He quickly scanned the parlor, waiting until Hough closed the door.

"Anyone else in the house, Judge?"

"Why do you ask?"

"We've had some trouble downtown. I need to talk to you confidential."

"I see," Hough said equably. "As it happens,

we're quite alone. My wife has choir practice to-night."

"That a fact?" Starbuck seemed amused. "No offense, but I wouldn't have figured you for a dea-con."

"Oh, why not?"

"Well, politics and God are sort of like trying to mix vinegar and honey. Leastways that's what a pretty smart fellow told me once."

"Indeed? Was he a minister?"

"A rancher," Starbuck said flatly. "The Kid killed him last fall, over in the Panhandle."

Hough stared at him a moment, then led the way down the hall. "Shall we talk in the study? If you care for a drink, perhaps you'll join me in a brandy."

"Thanks, but I make it a habit never to drink on duty."

"Very commendable."

Hough turned into the study, entering through wide sliding doors. Lamplight streamed across the hall, bathing a formal dining room in dim shadows. Starbuck, lagging behind a pace, gave the dining room a swift visual check. He noted a closed swing-ing door, directly opposite the entranceway, which he assumed led to the kitchen. He thought he de-tected the lingering odor of cigar smoke.

The study was paneled, with a fireplace along one wall and a gleaming walnut desk at the far end of the room. The wall opposite the fireplace, from floor to ceiling, was lined with English classics in red morocco bindings and row upon row of legal texts.

A matched pair of leather armchairs was positioned before the desk.

"Have a seat." Hough circled the desk, motioning him to a chair. "You mentioned something about trouble downtown. What kind of trouble?"

Starbuck remained standing. He pulled out the makings and began rolling a smoke. Hough was on the verge of sitting, then apparently changed his mind. He waited, one hand resting on the desk top, watching as the cigarette took shape. Starbuck struck a match on his thumbnail, glanced up quickly.

"The Nesbeths were killed about an hour ago."

"The Nesbeths?" Hough appeared bemused. "Are you talking about the couple who kept house for Joe Coghlin?"

"Them and their daughter." Starbuck snuffed the match and dropped it in an ashtray on the desk. A pile of cigar ashes caught his eye, but there was no cigar stub in the ashtray. He exhaled a wreath of smoke. "Somebody shotgunned the Nesbeths and a couple of deputies while they were having supper at the hotel."

"Good Lord." Hough shook his head with a rueful frown. "Does Garrett have any idea as to why they were killed?"

"Way it looks, somebody didn't want them testifying against Coghlin at the hearing tomorrow."

"Then you suspect Coghlin's behind it?"

Starbuck regarded him evenly. "Coghlin says you're behind it."

"I beg your pardon?"

"He says you could tell me who pulled the trigger on the Nesbeths."

"That's ridiculous!"

"He's also willing to swear that you're the one who ordered them killed."

"Am I to understand you're accusing me of murder?"

"Among other things."

Hough drew himself up to his full height. His sallow features appeared jaundiced in the lamplight, but his gaze was steady. He lifted his chin and stared across the desk at Starbuck.

"What other things?"

"How about conspiracy? Or cattle rustling? Maybe four or five counts of accessory to murder?"

"Completely unfounded! Not to mention the fact that you're relying solely on the word of an alleged cow thief."

"No," Starbuck said slowly. "Not altogether. You see, Garrett's out arresting Jack Dobson right now. I've got a hunch he can be persuaded to go along with Coghlin. That'll make it two against one."

"I think not! My only connection with Dobson is political. And as for Coghlin, I barely know the man. You're on a fishing expedition, Deputy, and if you'll pardon my saying so . . . you're not much of an angler."

"Well, for a man you hardly know, Coghlin sure knows a lot about you."

"Oh, such as?"

"Such as those monthly trips you take to Santa Fe."

"Those trips are certainly no secret. Everyone knows I have business interests in Santa Fe."

Starbuck took a chance. "In the back room of a feed store?"

Hough's eyes suddenly became guarded. "I don't believe I follow you."

"The Acme Grain and Feed. That's where you meet Warren Mitchell every month."

"Warren Mitchell is a business acquaintance, nothing more. From time to time, he advises me on matters pertaining to land investments."

"C'mon, Judge." Starbuck gave him a sardonic look. "Who're you trying to kid? Everybody knows Mitchell is the front man for the Santa Fe Ring."

"Allegations are cheap," Hough said blandly. "To my knowledge, Warren Mitchell is a man of integrity and high moral character. As for the Santa Fe Ring, I've always considered it a pipe dream concocted by a certain political element. A fairy tale designed to obscure the issues and smear the reputation of honorable men."

Starbuck laughed a bitter laugh. "You wouldn't admit anything if your life depended on it, would you, Judge?"

"That sounds vaguely like a threat, Mr. Starbuck."

"Take it any way you please."

"Am I to assume my life is in danger?"

Starbuck considered a moment. "All depends."

"Perhaps you could elaborate."

"I'm trying to decide which way suits me best. You'd suffer a lot more if I let them hang you. But the way the law works, that could drag out till who knows when."

"And the . . . alternative?"

"Well, after what happened tonight, I'm tempted to do the job myself. I'll have to say it would give me a world of pleasure, Judge. Lots more than seeing you hang."

"You mean here—now?"

"Better now than never, leastways from where I stand."

"An unfortunate choice on your—"

Starbuck heard the creak of a door an instant before Hough ducked behind the desk. He whirled, drawing as he turned, and peered across the hallway into the dining room. He leveled the Colt and drilled two fast shots through the kitchen door. Centered waist-high, the bullet holes were no more than a handspan apart. The door swung open, and Earl Gantry, clutching a sawed-off shotgun, stumbled into the dining room. Starbuck fired the instant he appeared, placing the third shot slightly below the breastbone. The scattergun flew out of Gantry's hands and he pitched forward across the dining room table. His legs collapsed and he toppled sideways to the floor.

All in a split second, Starbuck crouched and spun around. Owen Hough froze, his hand wedged inside the center drawer of the desk. Starbuck extended the Colt to arm's length.

"Don't get brave, Judge. Bring it out real slow."

Hough took a bulldog revolver from the drawer, holding it between his thumb and forefinger. He carefully laid it on the desk, each movement distinct and exaggerated. Then he dropped his arms at his sides.

"An impulsive act," he said weakly. "I'm really not a man of violence, Mr. Starbuck."

"You could've fooled me."

"Luke!"

Starbuck spoke over his shoulder. "In here, John. On your way by, check Gantry out."

There was a lull of several seconds, then John Poe moved through the dining room and advanced into the study. He halted beside Starbuck.

"Stone cold dead. You got him all three times."

"Guess I haven't lost my touch."

Poe grunted. "How'd you know it wasn't me? I could've slipped through the back door easy as not."

"You don't smoke cigars."

"What the hell's that got to do with anything?"

"A private joke," Starbuck said with a tight smile. "The judge thought he had me in a squeeze. I told him what he wanted to hear, and he gave Gantry the high sign. Worked out a little different than he expected."

"You set me up!" Hough flared. "You never meant to kill me."

"Oh?" Starbuck's eyes were cold; impassive. "I didn't say that, Judge."

Hough suddenly looked uncertain. "I have powerful friends in Santa Fe. Kill me and I promise you, you're a dead man, Starbuck! They'll hunt you down wherever you go."

"Yeah, they might," Starbuck said quietly. "But let's suppose you were arrested and brought to trial. Carry it a step further, and say Coghlin and Dobson talked enough to get you convicted. Do you think your powerful friends would let you swing, Judge?"

"I—" Hough stopped, his eyes filled with panic. "Yes, they would! I know they would!"

"No, they wouldn't, Judge. To keep you quiet, they'd arrange a commutation. Then in a few years, you'd get an executive pardon, and walk out a free man."

A quiet steel fury spilled over in Starbuck's voice. "I don't reckon that's an idea I could live with."

"I'll turn state's evidence! I'll give them to you, Starbuck! Mitchell and all the others—the Santa Fe Ring!"

"You should've thought of that before you had the Nesbeths killed."

"For the love of God—"

Starbuck shot him. The impact of the slug drove him backward into the wall. He hung there, his eyes distended and his lifeblood jetting a brilliant red starburst across his chest. Then he sagged at the knees, and like a limp concertina, folded slowly to the floor. His sphincter voided in death.

There was a moment of tomblike silence. Without speaking, Starbuck jacked empties out of his Colt and calmly reloaded. Then, his brow lifted in a saturnine squint, he glanced at Poe.

"John, we'll just act like all this happened while you were still outside. Anybody wants to argue about it, I'll deal with them myself. Understood?"

Poe muttered something under his breath. He walked to the desk, scooped up the bulldog revolver, and tossed it on the floor beside the body. Dusting his hands together, he turned to Starbuck, grinning.

"Crazy sonovabitch! Got himself killed resisting arrest."

Starbuck smiled. "Yeah, I guess he did at that."

CHAPTER 20

"We buried them yesterday."

"Nice service, was it?"

"Not bad," Starbuck replied, "if you like funerals."

Chisum nodded soberly. "Luke, at a time like this, there ain't a helluva lot that'll ease a man's misery. But I want you to know I'm sorry, most especially about Ellen. Her and her folks were good people."

"Well, all things considered, I guess they got a pretty fair send-off. Garrett arranged for a preacher, and about half the town turned out. Weren't exactly what you'd call mourners, but it was decent of them to make the effort."

"How about funeral expenses? I'd count it a privilege to look after that personal."

"Already covered," Starbuck told him. "I figured that was the least I could do . . . seeing as how . . ."

He left the thought unfinished, and Chisum eyed him in silence for a moment. "For whatever it's worth, it ain't gonna do no good to blame yourself, Luke. These things happen, and no one man ought to hold himself responsible. Life's hard, but it ain't that hard."

"Maybe not." Starbuck paused, considering. "One time I heard a fellow say it's people that haunt our lives, not ghosts. I never really understood what he meant until now."

Chisum merely nodded. Neither of them were overly sentimental by nature. Nor were they comfortable with philosophical maunderings. Death was no stranger, and both of them had killed often enough that they had come to view it with a degree of pragmatism. Watching the younger man, Chisum sensed there was no need to dwell further on the dead. He put a match to his pipe, and turned the conversation to a happier note.

"So Owen Hough pulled a gun on you, did he?"

Starbuck smiled in spite of himself. "That's the official version. Course, looking at it the other way round, you might say he committed suicide."

"Queer, ain't it?" Chisum puffed his pipe, thoughtful. "Him tryin' a damn-fool stunt like that?"

"How so?"

"I just never pegged him as the type, that's all. His kind generally ain't got the stomach to do their own fightin'."

"Yeah, generally," Starbuck said, with a touch of irony. "I reckon it was a case of him having his back to the wall."

Chisum gave him an owlish look. "Sometimes a man gets stood up against the wall."

"It happens," Starbuck allowed. "Sometimes."

"Naturally, you wouldn't have done that to Hough, would you?"

"Why, aren't you satisfied with the way things worked out?"

"Suppose you tell me."

"Well, we've got Coghlin and Dobson in jail. Coghlin's talking a blue streak, and more than likely he'll manage to get Dobson hung. All the rest—Gantry and Hough, the Kid—they're dead. I'd say that pretty much squares the account."

"Not altogether," Chisum commented. "Hough was our only lead to the Santa Fe Ring. Or had you forgot that?"

"Tell you the truth"—Starbuck smiled, spread his hands—"when Hough pulled that gun on me, it plumb slipped my mind. I never gave a thought to that bunch in Santa Fe till it was too late. Hope I didn't spoil it for you, John."

Chisum reflected a moment. "You much of a reader?"

"No," Starbuck looked surprised. "Why do you ask?"

"Well, if you were, you'd understand why I ain't too bent out of shape. Not that I'm a scholar, or anything like that; but I've always had a taste for history books. Taught me stuff that's come in mighty handy over the years."

"What's that got to do with the Santa Fe Ring?"

"Funny thing about history, Luke. The true-blue scoundrels hardly ever get caught in the wringer.

I'm talkin' about the men behind the scenes—the ones with *real* power—like that bunch in Santa Fe. One way or another, they generally manage to slip loose. It's the kings and conquerors that get their heads lopped off. The men pullin' their strings are goddamn near invisible—and untouchable."

"Are you saying you never really expected to nail them?"

"I'm saying, I ain't all that disappointed. We fought 'em to a standstill, and they're gonna stay clear of the Pecos for a long time to come. I ain't greedy, Luke. I'll settle for that, and thankful to get it."

"Kings and conquerors," Starbuck mused aloud. "Don't know why, but that puts me in mind of Garrett. When I left Lincoln, he was holding court for a regular herd of reporters. To hear him tell it, he's brought law and order to the territory, and done it with one hand tied behind his back."

"Guess it figures," Chisum grumbled. "Course, men like Pat don't last long. A little fame goes to their heads, then the hullabaloo dies down, and before you know it, they're lost in the shuffle. I'd say Pat's had his day in the limelight. From here on out, he's got nowhere to go but down."

"Too bad he thinks so much of himself. With some experience under his belt, he could've made a good lawman."

"Yeah, like the sayin' goes, a man's just askin' for trouble when his reach exceeds his grasp. If I'm any judge, killin' the Kid was the worst thing that ever happened to Garrett."

Starbuck uncoiled from his chair and stood. "I reckon it's about that time, John. The boys are waiting on me, and we've got a fair piece to travel."

"Where you headed?"

"The Panhandle. What with one thing and another, it's been a spell since I looked after personal business."

"Jumpin' Jehoshaphat!" Chisum laughed. "I clean forgot you're a rancher now! Lemme be the first to welcome you to the club."

"Waste of time," Starbuck pointed out. "I don't aim to be a rancher very long."

"Why not?"

"Well, I suppose it's mainly a matter of being tied down. I've thought it through, and owning a cattle spread don't make sense for a man with itchy feet. Lucky for me, there's a group of fellows over there that want the LX real bad. I plan to sell while they're still keen to buy."

"Then what?" Chisum's rheumy eyes narrowed. "You're gonna have more money than you ever dreamt possible. You given any thought to that?"

"No, not a lot. I'll likely squirrel it away in a bank and just take things as they come."

"Sounds like you mean to retire from the detective business?"

Starbuck was silent for a time. "I've got a taste for it, and I'd only be fooling myself to say otherwise. One way or another, I guess I'll stick with it."

"Good!" Chisum hunched forward in his chair. "Now I'm gonna tell you a little secret. Come next spring, there'll be an organization called the International Range Association. It'll be headquartered in Denver, and the board of directors will be made up of men representing stockgrowers' associations from every territory and state in the West."

He paused, frowning. "I had a hand in puttin' it together, and I won't horse you around, Luke. One of the reasons was political; we need more clout in Washington, and the only way that'll happen is for us to get our own men elected to Congress. But the other reason is right up your alley. We're gonna put together the goddamnedest force of stock detectives there ever was! They won't be hogtied by state boundaries or the law or anything else. They'll go wherever they're needed, and their one purpose will be to put the fear of God in cattle rustlers and horse thieves."

Once again he stopped, and this time he fixed Starbuck with a penetrating gaze. "How would you like to be the head wolf of the detective squad?"

"I don't know." Starbuck sounded wary. "I'm used to operating pretty much on my own. An outfit the size you're talking about, it'd be hard to say."

"Will you think it over?" Chisum demanded. "You're made for the job, Luke! I'll write the people involved and tell 'em to give you a free hand, no strings attached. Hell, if you want it, I'll get you a guarantee chiseled in stone! How's that sound?"

Starbuck smiled, nodding. "I might be willing to talk about it."

"Fair enough! You get your ranch sold and keep your saddle handy. I'll let you know when to contact our people in Denver."

"I'm available," Starbuck assured him. "Leastways I will be once I've got the LX off my hands."

"Before you go," Chisum said, suddenly solemn, "there's one more thing. It ain't likely I'll be around this time next year, so it's best said now." His eyes glistened, but his voice was firm. "You fought my fight, and when I check out, I want you to know I'll do it with my mind at rest. You're a helluva man, Luke Starbuck."

The two men clasped hands, staring gravely into each other's eyes. Then Starbuck walked swiftly toward the door. He stopped, almost into the hallway, and turned to look once more at Chisum.

"I'll want to hear from you, John. Count on it."

The old man nodded, unable to meet his gaze. He gently closed the door and moved along the hall. Ahead, he saw Sallie Chisum waiting in the vestibule. She appeared cool and poised, remarkably self-possessed. Yet as he halted in front of her, a wistful smile played across her lips.

"You're leaving us, Luke?"

"For now," Starbuck said quietly. "Don't want to overstay my welcome."

"You will always be welcome on the Jinglebob."

"I'll keep it in mind, next time I'm over this way."

She went up on tiptoe and kissed him on the cheek. "For your sake, I wish it had worked out, Luke. She loved you very much. So very much."

There was a moment of silence. She stared at him with a look of tenderness and warmth. When he spoke, the timbre of his voice was charged with vitality.

"I'll hold on to the thought, Sallie. It's the kind that'll last a man a long ways."

Starbuck smiled, gently touching her arm. Then he stepped past her and went through the door. Outside, the men were waiting where he'd left them, near the hitchrack. He exchanged a look with Poe, unlooping the reins of his gelding. He stepped into the saddle.

"Let's ride."

"Where to?"

"Denver."

"Colorado!"

Starbuck smiled. "By way of the Panhandle."